love among the shamrocks collection

Book One

Under the

Irish Sky

M. KATHERINE CLARK

Other Works by M. Katherine Clark

The Greene and Shields Files:
    Blood is Thicker Than Water
    Once Upon a Midnight Dreary
    Old Sins Cast Long Shadows
    Tales from the Heart, Novelettes
Soundless Silence, a Sherlock Holmes Novel
The Rest is Silence, an Edmond Holmes Novel – Coming Soon
Love Among the Shamrocks Collection:
    Under the Irish Sky
    Across the Irish Sea
    On the River Shannon
    The Land Across the Sea, an Emmet O'Quinn Short
Love Among the Shamrocks Collection,
      The Next Generation:
    In Dublin Fair City
    The Song of Heart's Desire
    Chasing After Moonbeams – Coming Soon
The Wolf's Bane Saga:
    Wolf's Bane
    Lonely Moon
    Midnight Sky
    Star Crossed
    Moon Rise
    Moon Song, a Companion
Dragon Fire
    Heart of Fire
    Will of Fire – Coming Soon
Silent Whispers, a Scottish Ghost Story

Dedicated to all the women who have looked for their Irish rogue

And to D.Q. Go raibh maith agat agus slán.

PROLOGUE

"Nessa!" he screamed. He was always screaming when he was drunk. "You let me in this minute, do you hear me?!"

Ness's cheek throbbed from where the back of his hand had collided with it five minutes ago. She didn't cry. He always said he liked it when she cried. Ever since the day she turned sixteen after her mom had married him, she had not shed one tear.

"Unlock this damn door!" He shouted. Then, to her horror, the door rattled. She knew he was trying to break it down but in his drunken haze, the hits were not as strong nor accurate as they could have been.

The lingering taste of his disgusting tobacco, booze, and nacho cheese caked lips made her want to vomit. She knew it had been coming. His smarmy, lustful gaze always rested on her a moment too long. She knew if she didn't stop him that night, he would do far worse than slap and kiss her.

She had to protect herself. The door was getting weaker and she could hear it start to splinter. Suddenly, she remembered; her grandfather had served in Vietnam. He had given her his old army pistol in his will six years ago. He taught her how to use it too and told her, should she ever need to, keep both eyes open, point, and shoot. Don't hesitate and make sure the threat was down and wasn't getting back up.

It used to be kept under lock and key under the kitchen sink, but once Tyler started his unwelcome attentions, Ness kept it in her bedroom.

Diving for her nightstand, she felt around for the cold steel. Her fingers found the grip just as the door caved in.

Screaming.

Point... Shoot...

Chapter

One

The sunlight shone through the slit in the drapes and directly onto Sean's face. Groaning, he turned over and buried his head into the pillow. When the sun's rays found his face again, he grunted and checked the time on the nightstand clock. Grumbling when seven in the morning glared at him, he flopped back over and covered his face with the quilt. He had just gotten home from his stag party four hours ago. Taking a deep breath and burrowing into the sheets, he savored the comfort and warmth of his childhood room and just about fell back to sle—.

"Sean!" He bolted awake. "Sean, wake up! You're supposed to meet ya father's sister at the dock in less than twenty minutes!"

"What?" he breathed trying to calm his racing heart and breaths. He vaguely remembered agreeing to pick up his aunt and cousin the day before but that was before he left for

3

the pub. His stepmother, Deirdre, of course remembered but he couldn't possibly pick them up now, not with his stomach roiling on him.

Grand, that's just what I need, he thought, feeling a bit soft that morning after far too many shots the night before.

"They're here for *your* wedding!" Deirdre yelled.

He was tempted to just roll over and try to fall back asleep, but his bladder wouldn't let him, and he was certain Deirdre would just keep yelling for him.

"Sean Patrick O'Quinn, get your arse out of bed!" And he was right.

Muttering a curse, he ripped the sheets off and rolled out of bed. Closing his eyes and clutching the footboard to steady himself, his head ached horribly. Once the dizzy spell had subsided, he found the white t-shirt he must have pulled off sometime in the wee hours of the morning and brought it to his nose. He caught the faint scent of detergent but mostly the smell of cigarettes from the other patrons at the pub and something the smelled suspiciously like malt barley. One of his brother's must have spilled a drink.

Eh, it's passable, he shrugged. Throwing it over his head, he hurried to the shared bathroom. Once finished, he decidedly did not look at his reflection in the mirror, nor did he turn on the lights. Ducking back into his room, he pulled on his jeans, also from the day before, and searched for his Converse shoes.

"Sean!" Deirdre bellowed. Startled, he jumped, banging his head on the bed frame as he blindly groped for his shoes underneath.

"Jaysus," he breathed and rubbed the sore spot.

For such a wonderfully sweet woman, his stepmother did have a rather grating and boisterous voice when she wanted.

After finding his illusive shoes, he pulled them on without socks and picked up his wallet and keys. Before he could stuff them into his pockets, his mobile rang. Looking at it for the first time since he woke, he was stunned to see several missed calls, voicemails, and text messages all from the same person. Trisha Reilly, his fiancée.

"Shite," he cursed. He had forgotten to call her before he fell asleep. Or at all during the party. She was clearly worried… or maybe angry. Deciding he could wait to hear her complain, he pressed the ignore button, sending a quick text.

Sean: Hey love, sorry I was out late, had a blast though! Will call soon, heading out on an errand for Ma.

Just as he hit send, he heard Deirdre yell down the hall again. "Sean, you're going to be late! Hurry up!"

"I'm coming, Ma," he called back exasperated. "Jaysus, woman," he mumbled. Yanking the door open, he squinted as the sunlight streamed through the skylights and hit his eyes.

Shuffling down the corridor, he braced against the wall for support.

"It's about bloody time," Deirdre stated seeing him walk down the hallway. She was in the kitchen cooking over a low flame. "You look a little worse for wear, there, Sean."

"Feel like it too. Couldn't you have asked Da' to help me out this morning?" he replied kissing her cheek.

"You offered. Phew, you smell like a distillery and that shirt smells like me da's cigs."

"You know Emmet won't let us smoke, Ma," he stated speaking of his older brother who used to smoke a pack a day until a few years ago when he stopped cold turkey. "It's secondhand, like."

"Aye, good." She turned back to the porridge.

"Where is da'?" he asked pouring a cup of coffee. Usually a tea drinker, he needed the pick-me-up.

"Where do ya think?" she teased. "With his mistress."

Sean had to grin. Deirdre hated that *stinkin' boat* as she called it. The old, wrecked, fishing boat was his father's escape from his wife and, when she was around, his daughter. Deirdre started calling the boat his mistress when Orin began spending more and more time in his shed than with her.

Heading over to get the cream for his coffee, Sean snatched one of the fresh scones that were cooling on the rack beside the stove. Deirdre slapped his hand away, but not before he had gotten a piece into his mouth.

"Mm, Woman! You can cook," he teased with his mouth full.

"Tiss, I've told you a million times not to call me that," Deirdre said, though he saw the smile that crossed her lips. She always told him how much she loved her stepsons, but she held a soft spot for Sean. Even at twenty-six he was still considered the baby of the family.

He leaned down and kissed her cheek again. She playfully and gently slapped his cheek away.

"Och, that's very hurtful," Sean winked. "I'll just have to up my attentions." He grabbed her around the waist for a big bear hug. Picking her up from the ground, he twirled her around.

"Sean Patrick O'Quinn, put me down," she banged the wooden spoon against his shoulder as she laughed. "You'll throw your back out and *then* what use will you be to Trish on your wedding night?"

He laughed at her bawdy tease. "Ya let me worry about that, Ma," he grinned and winked. "We O'Quinns never let our women down."

"Ach," she rolled her eyes. "Ya rogue ya."

"And proud of it," he kissed her cheek before he set her down.

He was the only one of his three older brothers and his da' who could handle Deirdre's mood swings. She was cursing and shouting one minute, and loving and sweet the next. Maybe it was because he was the youngest and therefore couldn't remember his biological mother as much as his older brothers did. But Deirdre was the only matronly figure he had, and he loved her as fiercely as any son could love his mother; biological or adopted.

"You look fairly shook, Sean," she said eyeing him as he made up his coffee and finished the half-eaten scone.

"That's because I am," he replied winking.

"I wondered. Ya didn't get in until three. All that stumbling around, I thought the house was falling down."

"Ah, nothing like, Ma," he replied. "Just had a great time."

"Your brothers did well?" she asked.

"It was grand."

"Will Trish's da' be there tonight?"

"Aye, he's coming up. Couldn't make it Thursday night."

"Glad you made a weekend out of it."

"Me too." He took a sip of his coffee and sighed happily.

"By the way, Trisha called me last night. She said you hadn't called her, and she was worried," Deirdre said nonchalantly as she stirred the contents on the stove.

"Yeah, I got her messages," Sean said. "I'll call her on my way," he snatched another scone from the rack.

"Tiss," she hissed shooing him out of the kitchen. "You're going to be late," she spanked his bum with a light motherly tap. "Get on wit ya. They're here for your wedding."

"So, you keep reminding me," he sighed suddenly serious, his headache coming back.

Deirdre stopped for a moment. He felt her gaze on his back as he grabbed his light jacket from the peg near the front door.

"What's that tone, love?" she asked almost cautiously.

"Nothing," he replied with a shrug. "It's just... I never did want the whole big wedding thing. I'da been happy with just you, Da', Cabhan, Emmet, Innis, and Sinéad there. I don't know... I'm doing this for Trisha."

"You want to make your bride happy," Deirdre smiled at him.

"I suppose," he answered turning away from her.

Deirdre wiped her hands on the front of her apron and walked over to him. Placing a hand on his upper arm, she pulled him around to face her.

"What is it, love?" she asked softly. He sighed and averted his eyes.

"Nothing, pre-wedding jitters, that's all," he answered forcing a smile. Then spying the time on the clock, he went on. "Oh jaysus, I'm gonna be late. The ferry will dock in fifteen minutes."

She nodded and cupped his face. Never had he felt so vulnerable. He didn't want his stepmother to worry about him but it was easier for the sun to shift on its axis than to get her to stop. She studied him, and he knew she saw everything, every detail he had tried so hard not to show. Fear, worry, and his worst feeling of all... questioning.

He was getting married in two weeks, he wasn't ready. He wasn't sure he wanted to. That was the worst. Marriage was forever, at least he wanted it to be. But no matter how much he thought about it, there was hardly any joy in his heart for the prospect of devoting his life to Trisha. Forcing a smile, he pulled away from her and kissed her check.

"I gotta go. Love ya, Ma," he said and grabbing his jacket, Sean headed outside to his car. He waved at his da' through the open shed door. Orin tinkered with the old fishing boat that everyone knew would never run again. But waved back at his son.

Getting into his car, Sean enjoyed the smooth feel of the leather seats and well-worn steering wheel. His brothers were all pressing him to get a newer car but Ole Bess ran just fine and had never let him down. She wasn't new when he got her, more like an ancient trophy that his grandda' had let gather dust in the shed for far too many years. There were too many memories. But his brother, Emmet was a good salesman and swore to get him the best price when and if he wanted to upgrade. But as Sean lovingly gripped the steering wheel, he decided there was nothing like her and he couldn't set her aside for a newer model. As usual, it took a couple tries to turn the engine over and start the car but as always, Ole Bess never disappointed him.

Pulling out of the gravel drive, Sean made his way to the docks of River Shannon. His aunt and cousin were coming down from County Clare to County Kerry and instead of driving the hours it would take to skirt around the river by car, they were taking the twenty-minute ferry across.

Sean let his foot press harder on the gas pedal as he gazed at the clock. Luckily his stomach felt a lot better after eating something and some coffee, but his head still pounded and he was certain his eyes were bloodshot. Pulling on his sunglasses that were folded over the collar of his t-shirt, he decided he needed to call Trish. While at a stoplight, he fished his phone out of his pocket and dialed, putting it on speaker phone in his cup holder.

"Where the bloody hell have you been?" Trisha shouted when she answered.

"Morning, love," he sighed, his headache did not thank her volume. "I'm sorry I didn't call—"

"Or answer or text or anything. Bloody hell, Sean! Last I heard you were going down to the pub with the lads for your stag party that was at three o'clock yesterday afternoon! I left you alone. I wanted you to have a good time and didn't want to interfere as I've been accused of doing," she spat. He sighed again. "But when it was on to twelve hours without even a peep, I got angry. I even called your mother," Sean didn't like the sneer in her voice when she spoke about Deirdre. He knew the women didn't like each other and he wished he knew why.

"I'm sorry, love, I didn't mean to anger you," he said. "Truth is... I was completely tanked last night. I honestly don't remember anything. Last thing was another round at the pub and then I woke up in my room this morning."

"Alone?" She questioned.

"What?" He demanded sure he had heard her wrong. "Of course, I was alone."

"Good," she answered.

So, he hadn't heard her wrong. "Shite, do you think I'd do that?" he demanded.

"You said you were langered," she justified.

"You know I'd never do that," he replied. "Why would you even mention that?" She hesitated on the other end. "After what we promised each other when we started dating, how could you possibly think I would go back on my word?"

"I'm sorry, Sean," she whispered, her voice fraught with emotion. "It's just, every scenario went through my head. I'm having my last dress fitting and Innis is saying you'll love it and all I can think about is you not returning my calls or letting me know what's going on."

"I promise, darlin', I'm fine," he answered. "Honestly, I just got drunk, like."

"Well," she breathed a laugh. "You're not the only one who did that last night."

"Oh yeah?" he grinned. "What happened? My brother take care of you?"

"What?" she squeaked. "Oh, ehm, yes, he made sure I was all right."

"Good," he answered.

"Where are you now? What are you doing?" she changed the subject.

"I'm heading to the docks to pick up my aunt and Keera," he said. "They're coming in for the wedding."

"Do we have their RSVP?" she demanded.

"Yeah, they're family though so what does it matter?" he asked.

"We can't just materialize food for anyone who shows up, Sean O'Quinn," she said heatedly. "You'd know this if you had come with me to the caterers and not sent your brother and best man in your place."

"Trish," Sean let out a long suffering sigh. "Look, Innis is great. He's really helped. I've been looking and interviewing for jobs in Dublin, love so we can have a future. I don't have time for everything."

"I told you. Da' said he'd get you a job at the shop," she said.

"I'm a teacher, Trish," he answered. "Not a factory worker. Not that there's anything wrong with it, I just… It's not me."

"Don't be like that," she snapped. "You can't live in your fantasy world forever."

"It's not fantasy," he gritted his teeth. "It's what I went to university for. You know, if we could just stay in Kerry, I have that great opportunity at the county school. We'd be set."

"I can't live in Kerry forever," she said. "You know I hate it there. I'm a Dub, born and bred."

He rubbed his eyes as he pulled into the parking lot at the dock.

"Look, we can't have this conversation now, I'm here at the docks," Sean said.

"There's nothing to discuss," she answered in her haughty tone. "I know you'll do the right thing."

He sighed, said *fine*, hung up, and got out of his car. The ferry was pulling in and the passengers were getting back into their cars. Flipping through his social media on his phone, Sean found the one he needed. It hadn't been too long since he'd seen his cousin, but Keera had been in America for four years at a university in Chicago. As he studied the picture of his cousin, he let every ill feeling and uneasiness drift away.

Chapter

Two

Seeing someone wave at him from the docks, Sean smiled and pushed off his car door. Walking down the paved embankment, he stayed out of the way of tour busses and made his way down the hill to his aunt, Siobhan who rushed towards him.

"Sean!" She reached him halfway down the hill and pulled him into a tight hug. "I'm so happy for you, love!"

"Cheers, *Aintín*," he grinned, knowing she loved it when he called her *aunt* in Irish. Her long flowing blonde hair was loose and fell beyond her shoulders as she stood eye to eye with his five-foot eleven-inch frame. Deirdre had often commented that Siobhan looked more like an Amazon Woman than an Irish lass.

"I just knew it!" she went on. "I knew you two would get married. Time you made an honest woman of her."

"Uh…" Sean sputtered at his aunt's statement. "What?"

"Oh, come now…" she grinned. "I was at University once… albeit donkey years ago…"

"*Aintín*, we've not…" Sean started.

"Oh hush," she interrupted. "I'm the favorite auntie remember? No need to hide anything from me. I know what happens. That's where I met Keera's father."

"Ugh, ma," Keera said walking up beside her. "Seriously, you and the whole college stories. It's really gross," Sean nearly laughed at his cousin's near complete lack of Irish accent and strong Americanisms.

"I'm just telling the truth, love," her mother said innocently, pushing a piece of Keera's hair back behind her ear and smiling.

"A little more of the truth than we wanted to hear," Keera teased turning to Sean. "Right, Seany?"

He grinned hearing her childhood nickname for him, scooped her up into a hug, and twirled her around.

"Jaysus, I've missed you, Kee," he said setting her down, her brown hair whipping his face with the wind. Stepping back, he grabbed their suitcases. "How's America?"

"It was good," she said, then turning, she called out. "Ness! Come on! We don't want you left behind!"

Sean's gaze followed hers to a young woman standing a little way off. Her vibrant auburn hair cascaded down her back. As she turned, the wind caught her hair and it flew into her face.

"Sorry," she smiled, her distinctly American accent caressed the word. "I was just taking it all in. It's so beautiful here."

"Yes, yes, that's what you said about Clare *and* Galway..." Keera rolled her eyes but smiled. Her phone dinged a notification and she pulled it out to answer the text.

"Well, yeah, I've never seen anything so beautiful. We don't have anything like this back home," Ness finally reached the group and looked up at Sean. "Hi. I'm Ness."

"Oh sorry," Keera replied putting her phone back into her pocket. "Ness, this is my cousin Sean, the one who's getting married."

"Congratulations," Ness said beaming. "I hope you don't mind. Keera's kinda stuck with me for a couple months and invited me along. I don't have to come to the wedding. I know it's really soon and everything is probably planned already."

"Nonsense," Sean answered. "We have another twelve days. We'll find a way to fit you in."

She smiled at him and something struck him like lightning. His gut clenched and his heart fluttered. He'd never felt that before. He studied her face with its soft lines, not as harsh as Trisha's and deep green eyes. She looked ageless as if she could be younger or older it didn't matter. But when guilt descended, he forced himself to look away.

"Let me call Ma and Da' and let them know we're on our way," he said.

He took out his phone and walked away from them. Trying to concentrate on his call, he couldn't help peeking at the redhead that was gazing out over the river. She was wearing skinny jeans, biker boots, and a thin sweater. She didn't wear a jacket but her delicate scarf hung tied about her neck. The wind picked up and licked about her hair, blowing it into her face. Swallowing hard, Sean's hand clenched with the sudden desire to push her hair back away from her face and kiss her. *What the hell is wrong with me? We just met for*

Christ's sake!

"Hello?" he heard his stepmother call from the phone. He cursed under his breath and raised the phone to his ear. "Sean Patrick O'Quinn, do *not* curse like that."

"Sorry, Ma," he answered. "I'm at the dock and got 'em. We're heading back now."

"Good," Deirdre replied. "I'll let your da' know, though I'm sure he'll make up some excuse to stay in that god forsaken shed."

Though he chuckled at her teasingly harsh tone, he glanced over at Ness.

"We also have another visitor. I'm thinking she could bunk with Keera," Sean said.

"She?" Deirdre asked skeptically.

"Yeah," he answered. "She's a friend of Keera's from University."

"American?" Deirdre's distain for all things *not Irish* was clear.

"Yeah," he replied.

"All right," Deirdre sighed. "I'll clear out another drawer for her."

"Cheers, Ma," he replied and hung up.

Looking back at his aunt, her eyes went from Sean to Ness then back again. He hoped with everything in him she had not seen the way he was looking at the American. His aunt loved to meddle.

"Ma's ready for us," he said hoping to distract her. "Da's working on his boat, so I don't know how much of him you'll see."

"I would be too if I had to live with that woman," his aunt said.

"Ma's great," Sean jumped to her defense. "Come now, Aintín. We all know you love her."

Siobhan snorted. "Maybe," but she finally smiled. "She did save my brother from loneliness."

"Da' loves her," he stated.

"Aye, I know it," she answered.

He breathed a chuckle, but his gaze fell back to Ness who was walking silently behind them. Desperate to hear her speak again, he called over his shoulder.

"What part of America are you from?"

Ness hesitated a moment. "Indianapolis," she finally answered.

"Oh grand," he replied. "The Home of the 500, eh?"

"So I've been told. Never been, unfortunately," she answered. "But nothing compares to this place." Once at the top of the hill she turned to look at the view across the water. The ferry was beginning to pull out of the dock and everything was peaceful.

After Sean put the bags into the trunk, he looked up and watched Ness. Something inside him twisted. *Jaysus,* he rubbed the spot on his chest where it ached, oddly, directly over his heart. *This is a new feeling*, he thought. Confused, he shook his head and called out to her again.

"We should get going."

Ness didn't answer. Not wanting to get any closer to her, he called her name and immediately regretted it. It felt perfect on his lips.

Turning a little too quickly, she tripped over her own

boots. Screeching, she held out her hands to brace herself but landed on her hands and knees with a thud.

"Ow!" She cried out.

Sean rushed towards her, knelt, and reached out to help. She recoiled and turned her eyes up to his.

"Where are you hurt?" he asked attempting to ignore the scathing look on her face.

"I'm fine," she replied through clenched teeth, not moving.

"Tell me, Ness. Where?" he demanded.

"My knees," she finally replied. "I'm all right. I've been through worse."

He eyed her. Her eyes closed, her mouth twisted, and her lips pressed together. "You're not telling me the truth," he said.

"I'm fine," she replied.

"I'm just trying to help ya," he answered frustrated.

"Thank you, but I don't need your help." Her tone was softer than he expected.

"Too bad. Come on, let's get you up. When we get home, my brother Cabhan will take a look. Make sure it's nothing serious."

"I simply got my feet tied and fell, it's not like I fell off a cliff," she said.

"I'd feel better if you'd let Cabhan take a look at you," he replied.

Her eyes searched as if trying to assess his motives. Truth be told, so was he. But there was something in her eyes that spoke to him. Something behind her eyes he couldn't understand.

Fear.

Accepting his hand, she slid her fingers up his forearms and latched onto the crook of his elbows. Sean couldn't move. His arms, his hands, his whole body tingled. Never had he had such a physical reaction to simply touching a woman. Everything she did, heightened his response. The innocent movement of licking her lips drew his attention and he mirrored her. He was transfixed where he was. On his knees, gazing into the greenest meadow he had ever laid eyes on. His hands clutched the underside of her elbows, his body leaned toward hers. Her only movement was to close her eyes and let out a small breath. He was so close, he could feel her breath on his lips.

The faintest touch and his heart screamed with elation, but his mind screamed with reason. Finally, he understood what his parents, brother, friends, and every book he had read was talking about; the immediate spark between two people. His father called it lightning. And he was absolutely right.

As he was about to surge forward and kiss her fully, his mobile phone rang. Immediately, Ness reared back, eyes wide, gasping. Sean reacted the same way and hurriedly grabbed at his pocket to answer the phone.

"Hey, Trish," he said, his voice shaky.

"Blue or green?" Trish asked him over the phone.

"Uh… what?" he asked.

"Blue or green…" she said again. "What's the first thing that comes to mind?"

"For what?" He asked, his brain not functioning properly.

"You don't need to know," she replied. "Blue or

green?"

He pinched the bridge of his nose with his forefinger and thumb.

"Uh..." he finally opened his eyes to gaze into Ness's and the dark green meadow had turned stormy. "Green," he said.

"Green it is... cheers," she answered and ended the call.

"We should go," Ness stated without emotion. Standing, she winced at the pain in her knees. Sean wasn't sure if he could stand but he nodded and forced his body to listen to his mind. They went to the car and he opened the door for her. Without looking at him or thanking him for the gentlemanly gesture, she slid in next to Keera.

"Everything all right?" Keera asked uninterested, looking at her phone.

"Fine," Ness replied and proceeded to stare out the window.

Shutting the door, Sean hurried around the car and got in the driver's seat. Starting the car, he was grateful Ole Bess started without a problem. He felt his aunt's eyes on him, but he didn't look over. If anyone asked, he was blaming it on the hangover, only... it was gone.

Pulling out of the parking lot, he knew it was going to be the longest fifteen-minute drive of his life.

Chapter

Three

When Sean saw his parents' house in the distance, he finally felt he could breathe again. He had heartily tried to stop looking in the rearview mirror at Ness as she stared out the window, emotionless. Constantly having to remind himself he was getting married in twelve days, he forced his body to stop reacting to the beautiful, troubled stranger. Once the car was parked in the driveway, Keera and Ness got out. Looking over at his aunt, he forced a smile.

"Getting cold feet?" she asked out of the blue.

"What?" he replied.

"You aren't that discreet," she said as her eyes went toward Ness being introduced to Deirdre.

"I don't know what you're talking about, *Aintín*," he said.

21

"Look, Ness has been through hell. She hasn't told Keera anything, but something happened in American with her adoptive parents. That's why she's here in Ireland, trying to have a fresh start, and you're getting married in a few days. You're my nephew and I love you, Sean, but please listen to me... Stay away from Nessa Alexander, for both of your sakes. It can only end in heartache for you both."

"I appreciate your counsel, but, *Aintín*, I'm not a child anymore," he said. "And..."

"What, love?" she pried gently.

"Nothing, just..." he paused.

"I know," she replied. "Trust me." She touched the back of his head and stroked his hair. "I just want to make sure you don't do anything to jeopardize your future, Sean, that's all," she said. "If you need to talk, I'm here."

"Thank you," he said. "I just don't know what to do."

"What about?" she asked.

"A lot of things."

"Talk to me," she offered.

Sean took a breath but shook his head. "I'll be all right. Thank you, *Aintín.*"

"If you're sure, love," she said but Sean could tell she knew more than she was letting on.

"I'm sure," he forced a smile that was as unconvincing as he felt. She leaned over and kissed his cheek as her brother and Sean's father Orin walked out of the shed wiping his hands on a dirty rag, a genuine smile across his lips.

Siobhan grinned at her big brother and slid out of the car. Sean looked up and caught Ness's gaze. He suppressed his protective side that had never reared its head before. She entered the house after Keera and he let out his breath. Slipped out of the car, he hurried to the boot of the car and opened it. Pulling out his aunt's, cousin's, and Ness's luggage, he heard his eldest brother Cabhan call out to him.

"Sean!" He turned to see his two eldest brothers, Cabhan and Emmet, came up to the car. "Feeling a bit shook today, are ya?"

"Shut yer gob, old man," Sean teased. "I'm surprised at your age you can handle more than one."

"The older you are the higher your tolerance level gets," Cabhan winked.

"And how does Rachael appreciate you flirting with those two tourists last night?" Sean teased. "Is her tolerance level high?"

Cabhan visibly swallowed making Emmet and Sean grin.

"I think our brother did not tell his wife, like," Emmet teased.

"I would imagine not," Sean replied. "And how was it for you, Em? With that woman who invited you back to her hotel room?"

Cabhan had stayed over with their parents after the stag party, but Emmet had snuck out of the pub with a pretty redhead around two in the morning.

"Those Americans," Emmet chuckled shaking his head. "I tell ya," he grinned as if that explained everything. "She was a dancer too," he winked.

"Come on, lads," Orin called to them. "Let's not keep your mother waiting."

Emmet latched his arm around Sean's neck and all three walked towards the house shoving and teasing each other as if they were teenagers again.

Everyone sat at the table and ate the breakfast Deirdre had prepared. She always said how much she enjoyed watching her boys pile on their plate and hearing their moans of appreciation.

"So, Ness," Emmet, the second eldest, started. "What's America like? How does it compare to Ireland?"

Ness looked up at him, his naturally auburn hair was a particular shade of dark red and lay shaggy around his ears. She smiled slightly.

"America, in my opinion, is beautiful, but we don't have, or at least I've never seen, anything as beautiful as Ireland," she said. "Unless you consider cornfields beautiful. That's where I'm from. The Midwest."

"How long have you been in Ireland?" Emmet asked.

"I arrived a little over a week ago," she explained.

"Kee said you'll be here a couple more months?" Cabhan asked.

"That's the plan," she replied, looking over at him. Cabhan nearing forty, was clearly the eldest. All three men, Sean, Cabhan, and Emmet had similar looks with Emmet being the redheaded Viking warrior.

"Have you seen much of Ireland?" Cabhan asked.

"Just Clare and Galway," she answered.

"Oh, that's a beautiful part of Ireland! Although, it's more hazy and foggy than nice weather," Emmet said.

"But it's what I expect," she replied. "You know everyone talks about the wet and misty bits of Ireland. It's accurate."

"Yeah, don't we know it," Cabhan interjected.

"Did you fly into Dublin?" Emmet asked.

"Shannon," she replied shaking her head.

"Ah, so you've not seen the city?" Emmet asked. Again, she shook her head. "Well, we're heading down for the weekend, I'd be happy to show you around if you'd care to join me?" Emmet asked.

Her eyes grew wide and Sean's gaze narrowed on her face. Again, there was something there, she almost looked afraid.

"Emmet," Sean said before she could respond. "You're not God's gift to women, leave the poor girl alone."

"I'm just trying to be nice," he raised his hands in a gesture of innocence. "Dublin is a beautiful city. There's a lot to see and I've been told I'm a fantastic tour guide."

"I would like to see it," Ness replied. "But maybe Keera could come with us?"

"Emmet doesn't bite," Keera smiled.

"Well, not often," Emmet grinned.

"You're terrible, Emmet," Deirdre said.

"Ah, Ma," he winked. "You know I love ya."

"That has nothing to do with it," Deirdre laughed.

Sean leaned closer to Ness and whispered, "I'll be there too. I could come with you," the words were out of his mouth before he could stop himself. She slowly nodded.

"Yeah, thanks," she whispered back. "Maybe we can convince Keera too?"

"I'll do my best," he answered. "I know it's gotta be uncomfortable to be alone with strangers."

"A bit," she smiled slightly. "But, I like making new friends."

Sean took her hand under the table and smiled at her. "Me too," he answered.

"Everything looks to be fine," Cabhan said after he finished examining Ness's scraped and bruised knees and hands. "Nothing too terribly bad, but you know, you should watch yourself, most girls fall for my little brother." Cabhan teased. Sean rolled his eyes.

"I just tripped over my own feet," Ness replied. "That's all."

"Of course," Cabhan said, his toffee colored eyes dancing. "I'll clean up your scrapes but there's nothing else that really needs to be done."

"Thank you," she replied.

"I'll be right back," he said heading out to the door to get his medical bag.

"How do you feel?" Sean asked.

"Sheepish," she answered. "A lot of fuss for nothing."

"Cabhan doesn't mind," Sean answered. "It's not often he gets a human patient."

"He's a vet?" she asked as he helped her stand.

"He's basically everything," Sean explained. "In a village the size of ours, you won't get an actual doctor unless you go into Killarney."

"I like it," Ness replied looking out the window.

"So do I," Sean answered. "It's peaceful here. Trish, my fiancée, wants us to move to Dublin when we get married. She loves the hustle and bustle of the city. But I..."

"You don't," she said simply.

"Yeah," he answered. "But, it's what she wants so I'll endure." He tried to smile but it was a half-hearted attempt and looked it too. His eyes drifted to the main room. Ness's gaze followed his. Emmet was on the phone, Orin was washing dishes, Keera, Siobhan, and Deirdre were sitting together chatting.

"Why would you do something that makes you miserable?" she asked.

"Because it's what she wants and she'll be my wife," he shrugged.

"That seemed like a canned answer," she replied.

He chuckled humorlessly. "I may have been asked that *a few* times before."

"But then why?" she asked facing him. "It's clear you're close to your family and you don't want to leave Kerry so why go to Dublin?"

"I enjoy Dublin. I lived there for four years while at Trinity. But every day I wanted nothing more than to be back here."

"I don't think you should give up your dreams just because you're getting married," she said.

"She has dreams too," he answered.

"Well, I guess I can just say I would never want my future husband to give up a family he was obviously very close to just so I could live in a city," she said.

Sean locked eyes with her. Without thinking, he reached out and slipped some of her hair back behind her ear. She looked back up at him, so many questions were written across her face.

"No," he whispered. "I'm sure you wouldn't."

"I'm sorry," she breathed. "I shouldn't have presumed. It wasn't my place to say anything. You two have your thing and I should never have talked badly about your relationship by saying what I would do. To each their own, huh?"

"What is it about you, Nessa?" Sean asked. "I can't seem to do what my head is telling me to do."

"I'm sorry," she said again. "But you should stay away from me."

"Why?"

"I'm... dangerous."

Sean's brows drew together. "What do you mean?"

She opened her mouth as if to speak but Cabhan came back in and she said nothing more as his brother prepped her hands with antiseptic and a bandage.

Chapter

Four

Once the dishes from breakfast were clean, dried, and put away, Orin slipped out to his shed. The women were catching up, while the Cabhan and Emmet headed home. But Sean was nowhere to be found.

Though he loved his wife, sister, and niece, Orin did not want to get caught in their conversations surrounding the wedding and gossip from Keera's two years in America. He shut the door to the detached shed behind him and took in the familiar smells, fresh carved wood, tar, and varnish.

He pulled off his Aran sweater and looked down at his t-shirt. Deirdre would hate it if he got the clean cotton dirty, but he didn't have much choice. Turning on the single bulb overhead, the flickering light illuminated Sean sitting at the work bench off to the left, leaning back in the old chair, his elbows on the desk behind him. He looked over as if he hadn't heard his father come in.

"Sean?" Orin smiled. "There you are, lad. What are you doing in the dark?"

"Sorry, da', lost in thought," he answered.

"So I see," Orin went toward him. ""Is everything all right, lad?"

"Yes," Sean answered leaning forward and standing. "I just… I needed time to think. I can see why you spend so much time here. It's peaceful."

"That and I have this," his father winked walking over to a cabinet and pulling out a bottle of whiskey. Pouring two glasses of the golden alcohol, he handed one to his son. "Do not tell your mother."

Sean smiled slightly but clinked his glass. "Wouldn't dream of it."

"Sláinte," he toasted. Drinking, Orin enjoyed the slight burn as it slid down his throat. Looking over at his son, who looked to be savoring every flavor, he teased, "a bit of the hair of the dog, like."

"Something like that," Sean replied.

"You seem to be better after eating this morning."

"I am, nothing but an acidic memory." Sean smiled but Orin could see it was forced.

"Something is troubling you, lad."

"I don't know," he answered on a harsh breath. "I'm questioning things."

"What sort of things?"

Sean hesitated. Orin waited and drank his whiskey. Finally, he spoke low. "Da, how did you know you chose the right woman? How did you know with absolute certainty that Ma and Deirdre were the women for you to marry?"

"Ah," he smiled gently. "That's what's on your mind, is it? You're getting nervous?"

"A bit," he answered.

"That's absolutely typical, lad," he said refilling his glass and offering it to his son, who declined. "It's a scary thing to pledge yourself to someone for the rest of your life. Trust me, I've done it twice. I never thought I'd remarry even though I knew you boys needed a mother. Then I met Deirdre."

"What was it about her that made you know?"

"Well, at first it was little things. Similar lifestyles, similar tastes. We could talk for hours and never run out of things to say. It was always new, fresh, and exciting. The butterflies wouldn't go away. I couldn't sleep for thinking about her. She would be the first thing I thought about when I woke and the last I thought of when I went to sleep. She would be the first person I would want to tell when something wonderful happened and the first voice I wanted to hear when something did not turn out the way it was planned. When we had a fight, my heart hurt that I couldn't talk to her. Or wouldn't as the stubborn case may be," he smiled. "I knew, no matter what I did she wouldn't get out of my head."

Sean's brows furrowed. And Orin watched as he worked through so many emotions. Staying silent for a time, he let his son think and sipped his whiskey. When Sean huffed, he broached the subject again.

"What do you feel when you're with Trisha?" Taking a deep breath, Sean didn't look at him when he shrugged. "When you think about her, what comes to mind?" he pressed.

"The wedding."

"What part?"

"The tedium of planning it," he replied. "The money put into it. The fact I'll be leaving you all."

Orin schooled his face to give nothing away. But he tried a different approach. "What about when you kiss her, son, what do you feel?" Again, Sean shrugged. "Do you ever feel like you have to stop yourself? You know what I mean."

"Do you mean, do I want to sleep with her?" he asked. Orin nodded. "Yeah, of course."

"Do you love her?"

Sean blinked. "I'm going to marry her."

"That didn't answer my question, son."

"That's just it, da'," he started sounding frustrated and turning away from him. "Everything you're describing I don't feel them for Trisha."

"But you feel them for someone else?"

"Yes," Sean answered quickly. "Maybe..." he covered. "I don't know. It's daft."

Orin thought back to the redheaded American currently sitting beside his wife in the family room and wondered.

"Let me ask you a question, son and I want you to be absolutely honest with me," he said. Sean nodded. "You know you can tell me anything and I would never judge you. You're my son and I love you. My loyalty is to you..." Sean swallowed and nodded again. "Do you *have* to marry her?"

Sean's brows furrowed. "What do you mean?"

"I mean, to be perfectly blunt, son, did you get her pregnant?" Orin asked.

Sean's eyes grew large but the innocence behind them told Orin all he needed to know. "No," Sean answered adamantly. "Da', I... I've never... with anyone." Sean's cheeks reddened and he looked down.

"I know it wasn't easy to abstain. I am very proud of you for resisting the temptation, lad," Orin said with no hint of embarrassment in his voice. He knew what his sons got up to and what they *didn't* get up to. Sean's announcement did not surprise him. "Tell me this, why did you ask Trisha to marry you?"

"I... uh," he stuttered then took a deep breath. It all came pouring out. "Because everyone was telling me how great of a couple we were and kept asking me when we're getting married and then *she* started to ask and then... well... it was just a lot of pressure. I guess I asked her because everyone said I should. I don't honestly think I thought of long term with her. We were friends in my opinion. Just friends. Sure we kissed once in a while, but I didn't... I didn't feel what I thought I should feel." Orin couldn't help the puff of air that escaped his lips. Sean studied him and then looked away. "That's not exactly the right answer is it?"

Orin didn't say anything at first. Anyone could see that Trish was all wrong for him. But Orin needed to know. He owed it to his son to ask.

"Tell me something, lad," he started cautiously. "When you think of your future... who shares your bed? Who do you see pregnant, carrying your child? Who is the mother of your children? Who do you come home to every night? Do you see Trisha?"

Sean stared at him for a long moment, then his face drained of color and Orin had his answer. A resounding *no*.

"Then why, lad? If you don't, how can you go through with this?"

Sean's eyes rimmed with tears. "I don't know." Orin pulled him into an embrace and held his son.

"Nothing is done yet that cannot be undone, Sean."

Sean nodded and cleared his throat. Pulling back, Sean wiped his face.

"Ugh, I'm sorry," he said.

"No, never apologize," Orin cupped his face. "You know how much we love you, aye? Your mother and me?"

Sean nodded. "Thank you, da'."

"Come on, wanna help me?" he motioned toward the old fishing boat.

"Do you really work on that all the time? I thought it was just a ploy to get out of the house."

"Sometimes," he winked. "Others I do like working on it. I know it'll never run again, but if I can help it look like it used to or better, then I will."

"I might want to have a shed in my backyard so I can escape whenever I need to."

"I'd be happy to build it for you. But until then, join me."

Orin turned to the boat, set his whiskey down, and picked up his old fashioned planer. Sean still stood by the workbench watching him.

"I'm going to miss you, Da'. I'm going to miss you and Ma so much when I'm in Dublin."

The tear in his son's voice caused a lump to form in Orin's throat. He looked back at him and smiled slightly.

"We're going to miss you too, son," he said. "It'll be lonely in the house when you're gone. But can't say I'm not happy to be able to have my way with your mother whenever and *wherever* I want." He winked.

"Gross, Da'," Sean chuckled but picked up the other planer and headed to the opposite side.

Orin grinned and settled into the rhythm of shaving and shaping the wood of the boat. He and his son worked in silence for a long time but Sean's confession was never far from Orin's mind. If he didn't feel those things for Trish, did she feel anything for him? And if he felt those things so suddenly for the new American girl, who was she and why?

An hour ticked by until both were called into the house to clean up for lunch. The stress had melted away and Sean was smiling and teasing his cousin as they sat together. Orin was going to miss his son, but he would miss him more if he knew he was not happy. Something had to be done.

Chapter

Five

Point... Shoot...

Ness heard her scream before she could stop it. Tearing off the bed sheets, she opened her eyes and for a moment did not know where she was. That is, not until Sean burst into the room in nothing but his boxers.

"Ness?" he demanded. "Are you all right?"

Orin, Deirdre, and Siobhan ran in behind him.

"Sean, what are you wearing?" his mother scolded him, smacking his arm.

Looking down, Sean must have realized what he was wearing and disappeared back through the door as Siobhan went to Ness and soothed her hair. Keera took her hand after scrambling off the other twin bed in the corner.

"I'm sorry," Ness said, her stomach still in knots and

sweat trickling down her back. "I didn't mean to wake anyone."

"What happened, dear?" Siobhan asked. Deirdre came into the room, turned on the light and sat beside Keera.

"I just had a bad dream," she replied. "I'm sorry."

"Don't apologize, dear," Deirdre answered. "We just want to be makin' sure you are all right."

"Sometimes I have nightmares," she confided.

"More like night *terrors*, love," Siobhan soothed. "What happened this time?"

"The same thing," Ness answered. Looking over at Deirdre, she went on. "Back in the States, I lived with my adopted mom and stepdad – her second husband – and one day he... an intruder came in and he was shot."

"You were home?" Deirdre asked. Ness nodded. "Oh, my sweetheart," Deirdre soothed. "How terrible for you."

Whether or not Deirdre knew Ness was lying, she did not say. But a look in her eye as she looked back at Orin in the doorway told Ness volumes. Sean returned, dressed in a t-shirt and pajama pants, and took a step into the room.

"I know the perfect antidote for night terrors. Join me?" He offered.

She stared at him but nodded numbly. It had been two days since she had last seen him, but she remembered the lightning that had shot up her arm as he helped her stand at the docks after she tripped. There was something about Sean that called to her. And yet, knowing he was engaged made her pause.

"Go on, love," Siobhan coaxed. "Sean is a master at soothing nightmares."

"Okay," she shrugged. "I mean, I guess. If it's all right." She looked over at Deirdre who smiled encouragingly.

Getting up, she pulled on a sweatshirt over her sleep camisole and headed after Sean. Stopping near Orin, she gave a weak smile.

"I'm really sorry to wake everyone."

"No worries, me wee darlin'," Orin smiled. "We just wanted to be sure you were all right. Sean will take care of ya."

"Thank you," she replied.

Siobhan and Deirdre watched Ness hurry into the kitchen behind Sean. Keera sat cross legged on the bed.

"Has she done this often, love?" Deirdre asked Keera.

"Yeah, Auntie," she answered. "The first time it happened in the dorm, I freaked. But she woke herself up and saw me. She told me the same story she just told you."

"What is causing it?"

"I don't know."

"Other than seeing her stepfather killed," Orin started.

"He didn't die," Keera replied. Then, looking at the three of them she went on. "I was there when the police came. They said he didn't die but left the hospital. The worst nightmare happened that night. She was so scared. Guys, I think something more happened. I think he tried to... you know."

The feeling of anger, sadness for Ness, and determination to fix everything lingered in the air between them.

"What can we do?" Siobhan asked.

"What about looking into it?" Deirdre offered. "Orin, don't you have a friend in America who works on the police force?"

"Aye," Orin answered. "Daniel. He works in New York. I'll send him an email in the morning."

"Whatever the truth is regarding her stepfather's death," Siobhan began. "Nessa is a sweet, beautiful, young woman. I do believe she is innocent in this. Let us not judge her too harshly."

"Of course not," Deirdre replied. "But I need to know who is under my roof and sleeping near my son."

"Of course." She turned to her brother. "You know I am able to sense the good in people. Our mother passed the trait on to me. Trust me on this, Orin. The girl may be lying about what happened, but I do believe whatever did happened was in self-defense and she had a good reason to do it."

Orin looked from his sister to his wife then back again.

"We all feel it too, Siobhan. Even Sean's been affected by it and you know he showed signs of that trait at a young age," Orin said.

"What trait?" Keera asked.

"Some people call it second sight, love," Siobhan explained. "You have it too. A feeling when you meet someone and have a vibe about them."

"Oh, that," Keera answered. "Ness is awesome. I really like her and I've lived with her in the dorm for over a year. She's grand."

"I'll send the email to Daniel," Orin replied. "Until then, let's get to bed."

"Should we not check on them?" Deirdre asked.

"I'll check on them later, make sure they haven't fallen asleep. But for now, let it play out."

"All right," Deirdre said then, with a *goodnight* turned out of the room and walked down the hall to her room, Orin behind her.

"What do you mean Sean's been affected by her?" she questioned as they slid back into bed.

"He told me somethings in confidence, love," he answered.

"Is all well?"

"As well as can be expected." Orin opened his arms and Deirdre slipped her head on his shoulder as his arm came around her shoulders.

"Is he happy?"

"Who?"

"Sean. With Trisha? It just seems like he's not himself whenever she's around. She dominates him and I don't like it."

Orin hesitated and Deirdre pulled back to look up at her husband. "What do you know?"

"Nothing," he promised. "Trust me, love." He kissed her softly, but soon, as usual, their kiss turned passionate and they lost track of time as they loved each other.

Sean watched Ness walk into the living room from the kitchen counter as he poured his concoction into two glasses; whiskey and ginger beer along with a dash of lime juice.

"Have a seat, I'll be right out," he said.

"What are you making?" she asked as she curled up on the sofa.

"It's my own specialty," he replied finishing with the juice and setting the glasses on the tray next to some cookies he found in the cupboard. "You do drink alcohol, don't ya?" She nodded. "Good," he smiled. "If you didn't, you soon would if Ireland has anything to say about it." He teased.

She giggled and the sound made him grin. His father's conversation in the shed two days ago made him think, he knew he needed to distance himself from her, she was making him question. But watching her, he realized he had never been lonelier than he had those last couple days.

Carrying the tray over to the couch, he watched as she wrapped her arms around herself and pulled her knees up; her cute pink painted toenails poked out from under her pajama pants. Picking up one of the glasses and handing it to her, he watched as she sniffed the sweet drink and gazed at the amber color.

"What's in it?" she asked.

"Whiskey mostly," he replied. He took his glass and tilted it to her. "Sláinte," he said. She smiled slightly and clinked his glass with hers. He watched as she tentatively took a small sip and then another. Grinning, she looked up at him.

"It's really good," she said.

"You doubted it?"

"Well, no," she answered laughing. "But I had whiskey with Keera, and I didn't like it."

"Well, love, you're going to have learn to like it while you're in Ireland," he said. "It's like water."

She smiled slightly, bit her lip, and took another swallow.

"May I sit beside you?" Sean asked gently.

She looked up sharply at him then proceeded to nod stiffly. Smiling, he took a seat beside her but remained quiet.

Finally, Ness spoke softly. "Where have you been?"

"What do you mean?"

"These last few days you've been MIA."

"Oh," Sean took a drink before he answered her.

"Did I do something?" she asked.

"Saints, no! I was staying with Cabhan. I stayed with Emmet for a couple days before you guys got here and then these last couple with him. It was nice, you know, staying with my brothers. Comforting. I won't be able to see them as often when I get married."

Sean took a deep breath at her nod, thankful she accepted his explanation. Though a white lie, he couldn't tell her the main reason for staying away was to not see her.

"Where's your fiancée?" she asked. "I would've thought you'd be staying together."

"Nah, she's at her parent's place in Dublin," he said.

"Where's your guys' place?"

"It's in negotiations right now. We haven't settled on the particulars. But it'll be in Dublin too."

"So, you guys aren't staying there before your wedding?"

He looked over at her and shook his head with an all too innocent smirk. "That would be kinda difficult since the family who owns it right now are still living there."

"Wait... what? I'm confused," she said.

"Oh... I see, you think we're living together?" he asked. She shrugged. "Ha, no. Didn't want to spoil the marriage with living together before."

Her lips shaped *oh* but she said nothing.

"So, do you have an apartment?" She asked after taking another sip. Her eyelids were beginning to droop and her back angled to rest on the arm of the couch.

"No, I don't have a *flat*," he winked.

"What's the difference?" she asked.

"Country."

"So, sue me, I'm American. We call 'em apartments," she smiled. He chuckled. "How did you two meet?" she asked.

"At Trinity," he replied. "It's a pretty big college in Dublin."

"Shut up," she grinned and slapped his shoulder playfully. "I know what Trinity is." He laughed. "So you met at Trinity?"

"Yeah, we were in a few classes together, then in a group assignment and we were walking together to and from class and residences," he went on.

She nodded, her eyes heavier and her head rested in the palm of her hand. Immediately, she was on alert.

"What did you put in this?" she demanded jumping as if she had been shocked.

"Nothing but nature's nectar and a lot of ginger beer," he said. "Nothing to worry about. Here, I'll put the tele on."

"No!" she scrambled to him grabbing the remote from his hand and staring at him. "They won't hear me if I scream."

"Why would you scream?" he asked confused but the look in her eyes made him pause. Making no move to take the remote from where she dropped it between them, he turned towards her. "Ness, I'm not going to hurt you," he stated. "I would never want to."

Her lower lip began to tremble and soon her whole body shook. Without thinking or caring of the consequences, Sean set aside their drinks, pulled her to his chest, and held her tightly. Finally, she let her tears flow and cried hard into his white shirt. Her silent sniffles connected to his heart. His soul cried out to hers. He wanted nothing more than to be able to kiss her tears away. Gently, he pulled back and looked down at her.

Trying to soothe her as her body was wracked with heaves, then hiccups, he stroked her hair back. Forcing the feeling that she was perfect in his arms, out of his head, he simply held her until she finally stopped crying.

"I'm sorry," she said wiping at her tear stains on his white shirt.

"No worries," he replied. "It's fine. Are you all right?"

"I haven't cried for a long time."

"I wish you'd tell me what happened to you. I could help."

"I can't," she shook her head.

He sighed, resigned. "All right. I won't press you. But you have a friend here if you want to talk."

She tried to smile. "Thanks," she replied laying her cheek back on his chest. His hand came up and caressed the back of her head. She closed her eyes. "You're very comfortable."

He chuckled. "Thanks," he replied.

"How did you get so good at chasing away bad dreams?" She asked.

"My sister used to have them."

"Your sister?"

"Mmhmm," he answered. "She's Da's and Deirdre's daughter."

"Where is she now?" she asked.

"Australia," he answered.

"What's she doing there?"

"School," he answered quietly, stroking her hair, coaxing her to sleep.

"Mm, will she be up for the wedding?"

"Yes, she's returning next week," he said.

When she didn't answer, he looked down. She was asleep. Adjusting her head so she wouldn't get a crick in her neck, he gently stroked her arms and started speaking Irish in a low soothing voice. Letting the sound resonate deep in his chest hoping the vibration against her ear would comfort her. Hearing her sigh a few times, he wanted to know what was haunting her dreams. Holding her tighter to him, Trish's face flashed before his eyes. He knew he should feel a sense of betrayal but all he cared about were the butterflies he had felt the first time he saw Ness hadn't gone away.

He lowered his cheek to rest on the top of her head and closed his eyes. She felt right. This felt good. He had never felt this with Trisha. Lightning as his da' called it, love at first sight, was another name, but whatever it was, he felt safe and happy and loved.

Falling asleep, he dreamt of seeing Ness outside with his family, laughing and teasing with them. She turned to look at him and smiled, such love emanating from her eyes. In his dream, Deirdre called her *daughter* and Orin patted her hand as he refilled her wine glass. Emmet was playing in the yard with a young boy Sean had never seen before, but he looked just like his brother.

"Sean," Dream Ness called. He looked over at her and smiled. "Don't be upset, baby. Trish and Innis are here." His brows furrowed but he turned to see his fiancée and brother coming up the yard. Trish, heavily pregnant, held his brother's hand in hers.

"What the hell..." he started.

Chapter

Six

"What the hell is going on here?" Trish's voice jerked Sean awake. His mind still groggy as he opened his eyes to realized it was morning. But the feel of something in his arms startled him. He was still cuddled on the couch with Ness. The thing was, Ness was now resting on top of him, his arms were wrapped securely around her, their legs entangled together. Ness woke with a start and gasped. Pushing off him, she curled up at the end of the couch. Sean cleared his throat and sat up.

"Trish, hey, love, welcome home," he said rubbing his hands over his face and feeling the stubble that had grown since his last shave.

"What's going on, Sean? Who are you?" She demanded from Ness.

"Easy, Trish, it's all right," Sean stood up. She pulled back and glared at him as Innis walked in carrying two suitcases. "Morning, Inn."

"Sean," but before Innis could say anything more, Trish cut him off.

"Who the hell is she?" she demanded again.

"This is Ness, she's Keera's friend from America," Sean said. "Ness, this is my fiancée."

Ness stood and smoothed her shirt and pajama pants. "Hi… um… good morning."

"American? That makes sense." She scoffed.

"Trish, it's nothing like that, honest," Sean tried to reason. "She had a nightmare and I was just trying to help."

"You were sleeping together," she shrieked.

"We fell asleep," Sean admitted. "But as you can see, we're both fully clothed and you know I would never do anything like that. Especially on my parent's couch."

Trish glared at him again.

Innis skirted around his brother and Trish with the luggage and, without saying anything, went down the hall to his room to drop off the bags. Running into his da' and Deirdre when he left the room, they pulled him into a hug.

"Welcome home, lad," his father said.

"Cheers, da'," he replied.

"I take it that since you're here, Trish is back from Dublin?" Deirdre asked after she embraced him.

"Aye, just. And there might be trouble in paradise," Innis said.

"What do you mean?" Deirdre asked.

"Well, I didn't see what initiated it but I saw Sean sitting on the couch looking like he just got up and some American curled up in the corner looking like she got caught stealing a cookie from the jar. All I know is, you could feel the anger in Trish," Innis said.

"Ah bloody hell, Orin you didn't check to make sure they didn't fall asleep last night?" Deirdre asked.

"Sorry, love we were otherwise engaged last night if you recall," Orin said.

Deirdre stared at her husband. "And who's fault is that?"

"Yours for being so bloody beguiling," Orin winked.

Innis suppressed a laugh. Shaking his head, he didn't ever want that image in his head but at least he knew his father was happy.

"I didn't think you'd forget that easily," Orin winked. "Let's go and see if we can help our son."

"Who is she, da'?" Innis asked before his father walked further down the hallway.

"Her name's Ness. She's Keera's best friend from America," he answered.

"Keera's here?" he grinned.

"Present and accounted for," he heard behind them.

Keera hugged Innis tightly from behind. Laughing, he turned in her arms and hugged her.

"Gosh, little Kee, you've grown up good," he teased. "I'm going to have to fight off a lot of lads…"

She giggled and hugged him again. His parents moved

past them heading toward the angry voice of their future daughter-in-law, leaving Innis and Keera alone.

"What's going on?" Innis asked his cousin.

"What do you mean?" Keera questioned.

"I mean your best friend and my brother were caught sleeping together on the couch by his fiancée," Innis said.

"What?" Keera demanded.

"Yeah, Trish found them when she walked in this morning."

"Ah, hell."

"What's going on?"

"Nothing as far as I'm aware. Ness had a nightmare last night. Sean made his tonic but that's the last I know. This is news to me," she said. "How did Trish handle it?"

"Not great," he answered. "She was yelling last I heard."

"Yelling?" Keera asked. "Shite, no! Ness can't handle it when people yell." Keera took off in the direction of the living room.

I have to get out of here... I have to find a way... Oh god, help me... Ness didn't see Sean or Trish before her, she only saw Tyler trying to kick the door down. She felt the sting of his hand across her face, the feel and taste of his disgusting mouth forced on hers, the loud banging at her door as he yelled at her to let him in.

Point... Shoot...

Covering her ears, she closed her eyes and screamed.

Chapter

Seven

Sean had never heard the kind of scream that ripped from Ness's throat before. His eyes snapped to her as she jumped from the couch and ran around behind it. She groped blindly for something, but stared at Trish with wide, wild eyes. Trish stopped yelling almost immediately.

Raising his hands, Sean approached her as if she were a wounded animal. "Ness," he called to her. Her eyes jerked to him. "It's all right. It's me. Sean."

Keera came running up and rushed to her friend.

"Ness, love," she soothed. "It's all right." Almost immediately, Ness's eyes reverted to the calm green Sean knew well.

"Ness," he tried. "It's all right, you're safe."

"Take a deep breath, love," Deirdre called gently. Ness

took two deep breaths and let her eyes wander from Keera to Sean.

"You're all right," he said.

She shivered as Keera pulled the throw from the back of the house and draped it across her shoulders. "Oh my god," she breathed. "I am so sorry."

"There's nothing to be sorry about," Sean said walking over to her and helping her stand. Keera didn't let her go either.

"You're safe," Keera coaxed. "You're all right."

"Thank you, both," Ness replied. "I don't know what came over me. I am sorry." Looking around Sean, she looked at his fiancée. "Sean is a good man. He helped me last night when I had a nightmare. I promise you nothing happened. We fell asleep, that's all. You have every right to be angry, but be angry with me, not Sean."

After a moment, Trish sucked her teeth and nodded. "Thank you for telling me what happened. I am not angry at you or Sean. I was just surprised by what I saw."

"I'm sure you were," Ness answered. "It was never my intention to cause a problem for either of you. I was," she paused and turned to Keera. "Keera, maybe I should go."

"Where?" Keera asked.

"I don't know," she answered. "Home."

"America?" Sean's voice cracked. "Absolutely not!"

"No, Ness," Keera shook her head. "You can't go back by yourself."

"I can protect myself. I have in the past," Ness admitted. "I can't stay here. I'm just causing more problems with your family."

"Trish is not my family," Keera replied.

"Kee," Sean groaned.

"You are," Keera answered looking at Sean. "But you are too, Ness."

Trish didn't answer but folded her arms over her chest and scoffed. Sean looked back at her and pleaded for her to forgive Keera. He knew the two women didn't like each other. Keera was never quiet about her distain.

"Ness," Sean turned back. "Listen, how about you go back to your room and lie down?"

She shook her head. "I don't want to sleep. Sleeping brings it all back. Is there somewhere I can go for a walk?"

"I'll go with you," Sean offered.

"No," she answered with a subtle glance at Trish.

The door opened and Emmet walked in. "Mornin' all," he called. When his eyes fell on the small group surrounding Ness, he paused. "Everything all right?"

Ness stepped around Sean and faced him pulling the blanket off her shoulders. "Emmet, would you come with me?"

"Where, girl?" he asked.

"For a walk?" she asked.

"Ehm," he started glancing to his parents then Sean. "I suppose, aye. If ye'd like." He smiled at Ness.

"I would," she replied. "Thanks. Let me change into jeans." She hurried back to her room and emerged a minute later in jeans and a light sweater that brought out the green in her eyes. Sean stared as the goldenrod color highlighted the lighter features of her hair.

"Right, well, nothing like a bit of exercise before breakfast," Emmet said stretching his arms over his head. The leather of his motorcycle jacket crinkling.

"Don't be gone too long," Deirdre called as they headed to the door. "Breakfast will be ready in an hour. Will you be willing to help me in the kitchen, Keera?"

"Sure, Aunt Dee," Keera replied, then turned to Ness. "Are you going to be all right?"

"Yeah, fine, thank you, Kee," Ness said with a forced smile. Heading over to Emmet who still waited by the door, she glanced back at Sean, a look of hesitation filled with anxiety lit her eyes. Sean took a step toward her.

Trish stepped in front of him. "We need to talk."

Shite.

"Outside." Her tone gave him no way out. Swallowing hard, he nodded.

"We'll be right back, Ma," Sean called. Glancing at his father, Sean took the strength he offered. He had to stand his ground. A good marriage was based on mutual respect, not one of them bowing to everything the other said.

Sean stuffed his hands into the pockets of his pajama pants and lifted his chin. He had done nothing wrong. He would not allow himself to be nervous.

Innis flopped down on his bed with a sigh and covered his eyes with his forearm. Why could he never stay away from Trish? Why did he have to go to Dublin with her? When Sean asked – more like begged – him to go in his stead, he should have said no. He knew it wasn't a good idea. It was too much of a temptation. *She* was too much of a temptation. Neither of them was able to resist when alcohol and flirtation were involved. One kiss. That was all it took. One kiss and a night of passion he would and could never forget.

She was so perfect. He still wanted her. He would have shouted it from the rooftops the morning he woke up with her in his arms, but she had begged him to tell no one. He could never betray her even if he hated his brother's face for no reason. That was a lie. He hated Sean's claim on her. But he loved his brother. He could never hurt him. It was a mistake. No matter how many times he said it, to himself, he couldn't believe it. It wasn't a mistake, it was perfection. She was perfection.

"So, what do you think?" Emmet asked Ness as they walked together up a steep incline. Jerking her head back to him, her eyes grew wide.

"Oh... well... I, um..." she tried to think but had absolutely no idea what they had been talking about.

"You weren't paying any attention, were you?" He stated sticking his lower lip out exaggerating a pout.

She had to laugh. He looked like a caricature of a big baby.

"There's that laugh," he grinned. "I've been waiting for it. Made me work hard enough."

"I'm sorry," she said. "I've had a lot on my mind."

"So I've noticed, *cailin deas*," he answered.

Indicating a stone bench at the top of the hill overlooking the river, he sat with her.

"This is one of my favorite spots," he explained. "I come here when the duties of being second born get to be too much." He winked.

"It's beautiful," she agreed.

"So, tell me, darlin', what's on your mind?"

"Nothing important," she shrugged.

"I beg to differ."

"I don't want to remember."

"What don't you want to remember?" He asked gently.

Sighing, she rubbed her hands up and down her denim clad legs and stood. "It's nothing, Emmet."

"Is Sean making you feel uncomfortable?" He asked. "Just say the word and I'll have a talk with him."

"Oh no," she answered turning back to him still seated on the bench. "He's been nothing but kind. I just wish that I could..."

"Could what?" he pressed.

"Nothing," she stopped. After a moment of indecision, Ness sat back down. "So, tell me about yourself, Emmet."

"What do you think I've been doing for the past half hour?" he teased.

Grateful he took her not so subtle change of topic in stride, she smiled sweetly. "Well, I'm paying attention now. She sat beside him again. "How old are you?"

"Thirty-five," he answered.

"And do you have a girlfriend?" she asked. He chuckled. "Several?"

"Is this an interrogation?" he teased.

"Well, no," she answered. "A man like you wouldn't be satisfied with only one woman."

"Am I that transparent?" he asked.

"I read people well," she said. Then, looking back down the hill, she sighed. "Should we get back? I don't want anyone to get in trouble."

"Aye, you're right. Dee will be furious if her breakfast isn't eaten hot," he said standing but still staring out at the rolling hills. "I've forgotten just how magical this view is."

"That is the perfect word to describe Ireland... Magical," Ness smiled.

"Yeah," he shrugged. "'Tis."

"Do you think a little magic will rub off on me?" she asked suddenly somber. "I could use some."

"Anything is possible, lass."

Offering his hand to help her stand, she stared at it for a moment. "Emmet," she started.

"Yeah?" he asked.

"I hope I haven't given you the wrong impression..." she said. "About my... intensions."

"Oh, you mean the walk?" he asked. She nodded. "No worries, love," he said. "I'm comfortable enough to admit I know for some, Sean's a tough act to follow. We're all jealous of him."

"It's not like that," she answered. "At least..."

"I know," he smiled softly. "But if you feel half of what he feels for you, you need to let him know... else you'll spend ten years wondering, if only you had said something before it's too late." He cleared his throat. "And then you might be walking with some young guy when you're in your thirties telling him the same thing."

She looked over at him and took his hand. He had all

the traits of the self-doubting, self-loathing, ladies' man she had seen so often back home.

"Who was she? The one who broke your heart?"

"She didn't break my heart, darlin'," he said her as they walked.

"I'm sorry, I didn't mean to overstep."

"It's all right," he sighed. "The truth is, I loved a girl once. Chloe, she was all right for me, and I was all wrong for her. I went through some… personal hardships… and I knew I couldn't bring her down with me, so I let her go. She's married now. Has two kids and a third on the way," he took a deep breath and sighed. "But I never told her how I felt. That is the one thing I regret far more than not taking her as my wife."

"You have so much to give, Emmet," Ness said. "Don't let your past experiences drag you down."

"What could I bring to a marriage?" he shrugged.

"Well," she started. "I haven't known you long, but you have a kind soul, a wonderful personality, and enough life experiences to never judge someone. I could think of any number of women who would jump at the chance to find a guy like you."

"You forgot to mention my insanely good looks, or my roguish nature," he teased grabbing her around the waist. She squealed.

"Stop! I'm super ticklish!" She cried.

"You should never have told me tha'," he replied tickling her sides as he held her to him with one arm.

Screeching and giggling, she tried to get away from him. Breaking away, she hurried toward the house but one glance toward the side of the house and she froze. Emmet, close behind her, stopped dead in his tracks too. Trish and Innis stood there. Trish had a look of sheer terror in her eyes as she saw them watching her. Ness didn't miss Innis trying to subtly wipe his lips clean of her lipstick. Ness looked over at Emmet, his brows furrowed as Trish ducked in the back door. Innis and Emmet stared each other down.

"Ness, go on in. Tell everyone to give me two shakes, if you would," Emmet said. Ness nodded and hurried to the front door. A quick glance back, she saw Emmet stalking toward his brother.

Chapter

Eight

Ness found a place between the two imposing figures of Emmet and Orin. Sean's father had insisted she sit with him and even though she initially resisted, she honestly could say she had a wonderful time getting to know him.

After everyone was served, Deirdre turned to Innis. "How was Dublin, Innis? Did everything get off smoothly?"

Innis choked on his drink of water and coughed. Trish's eyes snapped up to his with a look that could've killed. Ness glanced over at Sean but he kept his head down as he ate.

"Fine," Innis strangled out. "Perfectly all right. Wasn't it, Tee?"

"Yeah," Trish forced. "Perfectly."

"So, it was satisfactory, then? No complaints?" Orin

asked.

Innis swallowed hard but nodded. "I think it was a success."

"Meet anyone?" Emmet asked, his tone icy. When Innis didn't answer, his family looked at Emmet who continued. "Oh, come on. You seem so much more relaxed than before you went to Dublin. I've only seen that happen on the occasions you met a woman and took her back to your-"

"Emmet," Deirdre stopped him.

Emmet looked over at his stepmother. "What?"

"Now is not the time," Deirdre said.

"It's true and you know it. Who was she, Innis?"

"Would you just shut up?" Innis demanded. "You have no idea what you're talking about."

"I'm just saying," Emmet replied, his eyes like daggers.

"How about you just not say, then?" Trish replied.

Emmet stared at her not giving anything away but the way his eyes turned to an icy blue instead of the warmth she had received made Ness slip her hand onto Emmet's knee and gave it a squeeze.

"Damn," Emmet breathed. "Riled you both up a bit... didn't know better I'd say you two were together."

"That's ridiculous," Innis nearly roared.

"Absolutely. Ridiculous," Trish replied taking Sean's hand and shooting her eyes to Innis.

Twisting out of her grasp, Sean stood. "Ma, could I be excused?" he asked. "I have some things I need to take care of."

"Of course, love," Deirdre answered.

"Thank you for breakfast, it was very good," he said.

"Do you need any company?" Emmet asked.

"No," Sean bit out. "I need to do this on me own."

After breakfast, Ness went to the room she shared with Keera and found her backpack. Pulling out her phone, she turned it on for the first time since she had landed in Shannon. The multiple vibrations caught her attention. Thirteen text messages and four voicemails dinged in her hand. She opened the messages and covered her mouth to prevent a scream as she saw the name.

Eventually, with one last buzz, she read the messages and yelped. Dropping the phone on the floor, she rushed out of the room, down the hall, and out the front door.

The fresh air was bracing but all she felt was adrenaline coursing through her. Heart racing, palms sweating, and vision blurring, she kept running. *This can't be happening again.*

"Nessa!" Someone yelled after her.

Twisting around to see who it was, she shrieked when she tripped over her shoes. She felt herself falling fast. Not knowing what was happening, she clutched at mud as she slid down the hillside. She screamed. All she could think of was she didn't want to die. She heard Sean's voice, then his face appeared above her. He clutched at her wrist and held on.

"I've got you," he shouted.

"Sean!" She cried.

"It's all right," he yelled. "I've got you!"

"Ness!" Another voice hollered.

"Emmet?" She screeched.

"Aye, girl, I've got him," Emmet's face appeared beside Sean's.

"Hold on to me, Em," Sean ordered.

"Got ya," Emmet answered.

"Ness, twist your hand to grab my wrist," Sean locked eyes with Ness.

"I can't!"

"You can. You can, Nessa," he declared. "Come on. Grab my wrist." She tried and gasped when she felt her fingers wrap around him. Sean winced. "Ease up on the nails, love." She loosened her fingers, realizing she was digging into his skin. "That's it," he began to tug. Grunting under the strain, Sean kept his eyes locked with hers. "I've got ya."

Ness managed to look over her shoulder and saw a straight shot down to a shallow river with one small rock ledge sticking out. She screamed and held on tighter.

"Don't look down," Sean ordered. Her shoulders hurt as he kept pulling.

Finally, she broke the embankment and Sean pulled her into him. Rolling her away from the slope, he held her close to him. Sprawled indecently over him, Ness clutched at his shirt and buried her head in his chest. Emmet put one hand on his brother's shoulder and the other on her back.

"What the hell happened?" Emmet demanded.

"I – I – f – fell," she shivered against Sean's chest.

"You've been doing that a lot, love," Sean panted sitting up with her still pressed to him.

"It's not like I meant to. I didn't wake up in the morning saying *gee, I'm going to fall on my arse today and see who catches me just for shits and giggles,'"* she answered. Sean and Emmet started to laugh.

"Are you sure?" Sean asked.

"Seems like you just might," Emmet replied.

She started to laugh with them. "I know, I don't understand it." She couldn't control her laughter. Then tears started rolling down her cheeks. She shook uncontrollably. Sean and Emmet wrapped their arms around her, and she soaked up their embrace.

"Don't do that to us again," Sean ordered.

"I won't, I promise."

"Thank the saints we were here, love," Emmet said. "I saw you running out of the house like a banshee and Sean started after you. As soon as I saw you crest the hill I took off after him."

"Thank you," she gasped out between shudders and tears. "Thank you both."

"What happened?" Sean asked. "Are you all right? Did someone say something to you?"

"No!" she cried and from their reactions she said it too forcefully. "No," she calmed. "I'm sorry. I just... needed some fresh air."

"Right, and you're that pale because you needed some air?" Sean asked.

"We're your friends, darlin'," Emmet said. "You can tell us anything."

She looked down for a moment, then her gaze shifted to Sean.

"Did Trish say something to you?" Sean asked.

"No," she pleaded. "God, no, she hasn't said anything. It's just. I got some... some news I wasn't prepared for. It's what causes my nightmares. I'm all right."

"What the hell is going on?" Trish's voice came from the front door. "Get away from my fiancée, you bitch."

Startled, Ness jerked against them and hurried to stand, only her knees wouldn't hold her up. She collapsed into Emmet as Sean whirled to face his fiancée.

"Enough, Trish," he spat. "I've had enough of this. Ness is our friend. Nothing more. Apologize for Christ's sake!"

"I will do nothing of the kind. You've had your eye fixed on my man since you arrived. I know women like you."

"Trish, it's all right," Innis came up to her from the side of the house.

She pulled her arm out of his grip and turned to Sean. "Are you really wanting to throw this away?"

"Throw what away, Trish?" Sean demanded. "I'm not doing anything."

"I'm sorry, it's my fault," Ness tried.

"No, you're not taking the guilt for this, Ness," Sean stopped her.

"You must really be proud of yourself," Trish looked at Ness. "Stealing what doesn't belong to you!"

"Trisha!" Sean bellowed.

Ness had had it. But instead of speaking against the abuse, she turned and ran. It's what she was good at. What she always did.

"Ness!" Emmet called after her. "I've had enough of this. You're deflecting, Trish. Why don't you tell my brother what I saw you and Innis doing earlier? It's rich, Sean."

"Go after her," Sean said to him. "She doesn't know the area."

"Oh, I'm going. But don't let either of them lie to you. You deserve the truth."

With that Emmet raced after Ness. Sean turned back to his fiancée and other brother. The dream he had the other night coming back full force when he looked at them.

"What the hell is he talking about?"

"Nothing," Trish replied.

"No more lies, Trisha," Sean demanded.

"Fine," Trish shouted. "Emmet saw Innis and I by the side of the house. Innis was a little closer than Emmet thought appropriate, but it was because I had walked into a spider's web and he was helping me check to make sure the beast wasn't on me. You know how much I hate spiders!"

Sean looked at Innis who looked frustrated but didn't seem to contradict her story.

"Is this true?"

"Yes," Innis finally said. "It's true. Emmet accused us of all sorts of things, but it was entirely innocent."

"If you're lying to me," Sean trailed off.

"You know I would never do that to you. I have waited for you and want to be with you. You're who I am getting married to in ten days," Trish said grabbing his hand.

"Then I need you to stop being bridezilla, all right?" Sean demanded.

"I thought you liked my passionate side," she whispered sultrily.

Innis went pale beside her, but Sean ignored him. "Just stop, Trish. This whole thing is giving me a headache."

"Come with me then," Trish said. "Let me get you some medicine and some ice. I want to talk to you. Just us. It's been too long."

He forced his mind to accept that she was telling the truth even though he was sure she wasn't. With a breath, he nodded. He needed to start treating her the way he was expected to, also, he missed her. They used to be best friends. He missed who she used to be. It used to be so easy with her.

Passing his brother, he took her arm in his and kissed her. Keeping his eyes open as his lips touched hers, he looked over at his brother. Innis looked away sharply and clenched his hand. His chest heaving with suppressed anger. Sean could understand falling for her. She and Innis were alone together making wedding decisions, Innis would have to be a monk to not find it alluring. Still, Sean pulled back and walked with Trish back into the house.

If they were lying to him, he wasn't sure they would like the consequences. As his father said, nothing was done yet that couldn't be undone. And he would leave them both to it if he found out the truth in time.

"Sean!" Keera called as they walked in. Hurrying over to him, she looked at Trish.

"I'll get you the ice," Trish said and went into the kitchen, leaving Sean and his cousin along.

"What's up, Kee?"

"I found this in our room." She produced a mobile phone. "It was buzzing on the floor. It's Ness's."

Sean looked at the smart phone as it lit up in her hand

again. "All right," he said unsure why she would share it with him.

"Take a look," she coaxed.

Keera handed him the phone. Swiping at the notifications drop down on the lock screen, Sean read portions of her received text messages.

Tyler: Where are you?

Tyler: Do you really think you got rid of me?

Tyler: You didn't succeed.

Tyler: I will find you.

Tyler: I always thought you were seasick. You look rather perfect on this ferry.

Tyler: You look hot in biker boots by the way.

Tyler: You can't get away from me.

Tyler: I'll always find you.

Tyler: Come to daddy...

"There's some pretty sick stuff on here," Sean said.

"Yeah, it's just that Tyler guy? I'm pretty sure it's her stepfather."

"The one who was shot?" Sean asked.

Keera nodded. "What if he tried to... you know, and Ness was the one who shot him?"

"Could she do that?" Sean asked. "Is she capable?"

"Anyone would be in the right circumstances. And something like self-defense? Hell yeah."

Sean nodded slowly, a plan forming in his mind. "Kee, let me keep this." He indicated the phone. "Don't tell Ness I have it. We need to get to the bottom of this and soon."

"Agreed. Everything okay?" she asked looked over at Trish coming back over to them.

"Aye," Sean replied. "Trust me."

Keera smiled and nodded. "Always."

Sean watched as Keera took out her phone and, turning toward the door, she called over her shoulder. "I'm going out. Be back in a bit."

"Out?" Her mother called. "Where are you going?"

His Aunt Siobhan followed her daughter out of the house still asking questions as Trish finally reached him with two tablets of pain medicine and a bag of ice.

"I'm really sorry, Sean. I don't know what came over me," she said as they sat together on the couch. Sean wrapped his arm around her shoulders.

"I'm marrying *you*," he replied. "For better or for worse, we will pledge to each other. We've pledged it when I proposed. I do love you, Trish, you know that, right?"

"I do," she answered kissing him lightly. "I'm sorry for being a bitch."

"As long as you acknowledge it," he grinned.

She elbowed him playfully in the ribs as she gasped fake indignation. That was his best friend. He had missed her. But when she kissed him again and turned her affections more amorous, he felt nothing, at least not the burning lightning that lit within him every time he saw Ness. Hating himself for it, he kissed her back, he pulled away placing the ice on him alternating between his throbbing temple and his aching shoulder. Trish snuggled into him and flicked through the channels on the tele. Ness never far from his thoughts.

Chapter

Nine

"Ness! Will you slow down, girl! Give this old man a break! I'm thirty-five. Not as spry as you are," Emmet called. She had reached the pinnacle of the hill they had climbed earlier that morning. Panting and sweaty, a good run was exactly what she had needed even though her chest protested. She turned to stare out at the mountain range in the distance. Though Emmet looked to be in excellent shape with a figure rarely seen outside of movies, he huffed his way up the steep incline and eventually reached her. He let out a comically exaggerated sigh. "Bloody hell... damn mid-thirties," he breathed.

"You didn't have to follow me, Emmet," she said.

"See that's where you're wrong, love," he replied. "I figured you'd need someone to boss around. We could run away together. I'm thinking elopement sounds good then we can start a family within the year... what'd ya say? Emmet

Junior?"

She stared at him as he cracked a boyish smirk and his eyes lit up playfully. She couldn't help but burst out laughing.

"There's that laugh," he winked.

Stepping forward, he pulled her into him when her laughing turned hysterical. Her head came to the middle of his chest and her arms wrapped around his broad back. She finally felt safe, protected, and cared for. He held her tightly.

Breathing him in, he wore a musky cologne that complimented him. The scent grounded her as her emotions ran high. Focusing on the smell of pine, she clutched at the leather biker jacket he wore over his muscular frame. His stubbly jaw scraped against her red hair, oddly comforting. The soothing feel of his chest rising and falling with his every breath and the solid pound of his heartbeat beneath her ear, gave her something to focus on when all she wanted to do was let the void of fear consume her.

Eventually her hysterics calmed, and she pulled away from him. He let his arms loosen only slightly as she soothed the wrinkles she had created by clutching his shirt. He stilled her fingers with his hand.

"No worries," he whispered. She tried to smile at him, but it was a feeble attempt. "Come, sit with me." He indicated the edge of the hill.

She wasn't sure if she could move, but Emmet guided her towards the spot and helped her down. He didn't say anything, and she was in no mood for a confession. Silence stretched.

Leaning back on his hands, he gazed out at the landscape before him. "You know, there is nothing about this view I would change. It's incredible."

"It is," she agreed. "It's so... green."

"It is that, love," he replied. "Have you seen many places in Ireland?"

"I've seen the Cliffs, a really cold and wet beach, thatched cottages, and sheep. What else is there?" she teased feeling better and hoping he would forget the mess of the previous few hours.

"True," he barked a laugh. "Then, I guess you've seen everything, back to America wit ye," he winked as he knocked his shoulder against hers.

She laughed but, after a moment, looked down. "Maybe America is where I belong," she mumbled.

"Ness, won't you tell me what's bothering you?"

"I can't, Emmet," she replied.

He paused. "Well, I want to know whatever ghosts are haunting you, I can help fight. We already set boundaries. I'm not expecting anything in return. But, I can help as a friend."

"Thank you," she answered. "I can't deny there's not something in my past. You've already seen some of the consequences, but I can never put anyone else in harm's way."

"I don't know if you noticed, love. I can take care of myself. I'm a big boy."

Ness smiled tiredly. "I have noticed. But trust me. If and when it becomes absolutely necessary, I promise I will tell you."

"I can accept that. But I would help and protect you as much as I can. I will never push you to tell me."

"Thank you, Emmet," she said.

Again they allowed silence to stretch between them. At last, Emmet spoke again. "Tell me, if there was one place in all of Ireland you would be wanting to see, what would it be?"

"Anything?"

"Anything, anywhere."

"Blarney. I'd like to see the Blarney Stone."

"Ah, Cork, is it?" he smiled. "That's our neighbor, you know. It's not that far of a drive. We could go tomorrow."

"Really?" She asked.

"Of course," he answered grinning. "It can be just us two or, if you'd be more comfortable, we can have the others join us. But I promise I won't take advantage of ye," he winked.

"I wouldn't be opposed to it just being us," she said. "I trust you."

"And I would never want to break that trust. One thing my parents instilled in me."

She rested her head on his shoulder.

"Why would you be wanting to go see Blarney of all places?" He finally asked.

She didn't say anything for a while and when he looked down at her, she bit her lower lip as a blush crept up to her cheeks.

"Oh, come now," he said. "That smirk tells of a story... Let's be havin' it, miss."

"It's really nothing," she said.

"I don't believe you," he pressed.

"Well, if you must know..." she started.

"Oh, I must," Emmet answered.

"I read about it," she started and then dropped her voice to a mumble. "In an Irish romance novel I read on the plane over here..." Emmet cackled and then burst out into a full belly laugh. "It's not funny," she defended giggling. "It was actually a very good book."

"Tell me, lass," he started and leaned into her. "Did the leading man have a phenomenal body?" she nodded. "Did he have an Irish accent that made the heroine swoon?" she nodded again. "And did this heroine and her Irish hero endure trials and tribulations before they were allowed to be together?" again, she nodded. "And in the end, did they live happily ever after?"

She couldn't resist and said sardonically, "so, you read romance novels. Good to know."

He laughed once. "Not me, my ex-fiancée."

"Oh," her stomach dropped, and voice hitched. "Sorry."

"Don't be," he answered. "She read more than her fair share of romance novels. We even playacted a few scenes." Heat rushed to her face, but she giggled. "It just seemed funny to me how every book she read had pretty much the same cover, a half-naked man and some castle or landscape, and the same plot. But, she never read one where Blarney featured."

"It was set in Cork and Blarney was where the hero and heroine met," she explained.

"So, you're hoping to meet your Prince Charming while kissing the stone?"

"I'll not be kissing any stone, thank you very much, Mr. O'Quinn," she promised.

"It's a good thing I'll be right beside ya," he replied. "Because if we're going to Blarney Castle, you'll be kissing the stone."

"You can't make me," she stuck her tongue out at him like a playful child then grinned as he chuckled.

Sitting in sudden, but comfortable silence, they gazed out at the scenery that stretched before them.

"I pulled out my phone from my bag for the first time since I landed," she began softly. Emmet stayed silent. "I had some rather... unpleasant text messages from someone I never thought I'd see again."

"Someone from America?" he asked.

She nodded. "It frightened me," she admitted. "That's why I ran out of the house."

He put a comforting arm around her and pulled her into him. She rested her head back on his shoulder.

"Don't ever be frightened, not with Sean and me around, love," he said. "We'd never let anything happen to you."

She closed her eyes. "No one's ever said that to me before."

"Then it's time someone did," he replied. "You're safe, Nessa. No one can harm you, not while I'm here. Especially not someone over in America." Closing his arms around her, he held her tightly to his chest, but the last text resounded in her mind.

Tyler: You can never escape me. I will always be there. Either in America... or here in Ireland.

A long time since any of the O'Quinns had gone sightseeing as tourists in their own country, when Emmet announced the idea, nearly everyone agreed to join them.

Sean's eyes sparkled with the idea of going to one of his favorite landmarks and it wasn't until Trish threw a fit that he agreed to stay behind. Orin eventually stepped in and spoke to his future daughter-in-law.

"I want this to be a family trip, Trisha," he began. "I know you have a few things still to take care of, but a day of family fun before you get married would build excitement."

"I don't expect you to understand, Orin, but my wedding is in ten days," there was an audible gasp and Trish had the nous to look immediately contrite. Orin pulled himself up to his full height and Ness then realized where Emmet got his physique.

"And I don't expect you to understand country manners, woman. You are marrying *my* son. You are in *my* home. You *will* treat me with respect, or you can leave this minute." Orin did not raise his voice, but the tone was unforgiving.

Everyone remained quiet as Ness glanced over at Sean, his face was unreadable.

Trish looked down. "I didn't mean to speak to you like that, Mr. O'Quinn. You have been nothing but welcoming and I do apologize. I am under a lot of stress but that does not excuse my behavior. If you would like me to leave, I understand entirely." She turned to Sean. "I am sorry, Sean."

"I do not want you to leave, Trish. But remember where you are and who you are speaking to," Orin said. "We would, I'm sure, like it if you came with us. But one way or the other, *Sean* will be coming with us if he wants to."

"I appreciate the offer, but I cannot. I have to call the caterers and florists. There's also the schedule with Placido our dance instructor. I have too much to do," she explained.

"I'll stay," all eyes turned to Innis. Stepping up to be next to Trish, he looked up at his father. "I know what she needs, let Sean go with everyone. Trish and I can handle this together."

"I don't want anyone speaking for me," Sean said.

"I didn't mean it like that," Innis answered. "But I don't really need or want to go. I've been there. Besides it might take longer to bring you up to speed with everything. I know what's going on. I can easily help."

"Fine," Sean replied. "You good with Innis staying?" Trish nodded but Ness noticed she went a little pale.

A knock at the door and then Cabhan poked his head in. "Mornin'," he said.

Everyone greeted him as he entered the house followed by his two young children, Lachlan and Fiona. Running to their grandparents, the children's squeals took the attention away from what just happened.

"I never thought it would be such a soap opera drama," Ness whispered to Emmet.

"Welcome to the O'Quinns," Emmet teased pulling her into a side hug.

Cabhan stretched out in the third seat of Emmet's jeep. His children rode with his parents to give him a break from *playing da'*. Keera and Sean shared the backseat, but Keera popped in her earbuds a half hour into the trip and pulled out her phone. Emmet insisted Ness sit with him so he could show her all the breathtaking views on the way.

Ness's phone was burning a hole in Sean's pocket and the texts he had read bothered him. He wanted to know the story and who Tyler was. He didn't know how to ask or if he even should. His mind turned to Trish and the wedding. The supernatural calming effect Innis had on her bothered him more. Their relationship worried him. They were far too close.

Sean and Trish had promised each other long ago they would keep themselves pure for their wedding night. He trusted his fiancée. But he wasn't so sure she had kept her end of the agreement. Shaking his head, he told himself he didn't care about her past as long as she was with only him after the wedding.

That was a lie.

If she had cheated on him with his brother, he could never forgive her.

Ness's laugh drew his attention. Looking at her was like staring into the sun. He was at war with himself. On one hand, he and Trish had known each other for years, on the other, he never felt what he felt for Ness with her. It was a quandary.

"Uh oh," Emmet's voice echoed in the cabin of the car. Sean looked up to see his brother's eyes in the rearview mirror looked straight at him. "Sean's in a mood. Maybe some music might help." Emmet reached for the radio.

"I'm not in a mood," Sean replied. Ness turned to look at him. She had an easy smile on her face and her eyes glittered. "I'm just wondering, maybe I *should* have stayed with Trish."

"Innis has got her well in hand, Sean," Emmet stated. "You need a little break."

"I haven't been doing anything," he admitted not liking the feeling stirring in his gut.

"I'm sure Innis is fulfilling *all* her needs," Emmet

replied. There was an edge to his brother's tone Sean couldn't quite discern but he heard Cabhan stifle a snicker behind him.

His brothers didn't know of his vow with Trish. They certainly didn't know he was a virgin and they never would.

"I'm sure it's not the same," Sean replied.

"I'm sure it's not," Emmet answered. Cabhan snickered again. "So... Blarney. I figured since we were only an hour away, we could show her the Rock of Cashel and stopover in Cashel town for dinner and a pint."

"Sounds good to me," Cabhan replied. "I told Rachael I'd send the kids home with da' and Deirdre."

"What's the Rock of Cashel?" Ness asked.

"A big rock," Emmet teased.

"Really?"

"Nah it's an old castle that was turned into a monastery back in the... thirteenth? Yeah, twelfth or thirteenth century. It's said to have been much older than that but the current structure dates back to the thirteen hundreds."

"You should've been a tour guide, Emmet," Keera voiced. "This stuff is so boring. Wake me when we get the Blarney." She rested her head against a pillow she had brought with her and closed her eyes.

"Boring?" Ness repeated flabbergasted. "I love it! Keep going, Emmet. Tell me more. I want to hear about Blarney too."

"What, didn't your romance novel cover it?" Emmet teased.

"Not as much as I would have liked," she giggled. "I wanted to go to school for British and Celtic history but I don't know Gaelic so I couldn't get in."

"You don't know Gaelic?" Emmet asked pretending shock. "Well, Sean... sounds like another pupil for you."

She whirled in her seat and stared at him.

"You speak Gaelic?" she asked.

"Unfortunately, no one speaks Gaelic anymore. I can read it and I speak *Irish* fluently," Sean explained. "Gaelic is an older version of Irish not many people know it anymore."

"Don't let him fool you, girl," Emmet said. "He knows everything about it. He went to school for it. He wanted to be a *Muinteoir*."

"What's that?" she asked.

"It's a term for someone who speaks and teaches Gaelic," Emmet explained.

"You wanted to be a teacher?" she asked Sean.

"I actually am a teacher," he replied with a shrug. "I was asked to be Head Teacher at one of the local primary schools when it's back in session."

"That's great!" she said.

He smiled sadly. "Unfortunately, as soon as Trish and I are married, I'll have to let them know I won't be able to accept. She wants to move to Dublin and it's too far for me to commute daily."

Ness's brows pulled together. "You'd give up your dream to move to Dublin?"

"It's what Trish wants," he answered. "And there are several schools in Dublin. I might even be able to teach at Trinity."

"Do you *want* to teach in Dublin?" She asked.

He locked eyes with her and smiled slightly.

"I make the best out of any situation," he admitted. They stared at each other for a long moment. But he didn't miss Emmet looking at Cabhan in the rearview mirror.

Pulling to a stop in the parking lot of Blarney town, Tyler watched as Ness and the others gathered around the cars. Ness's gaze trailed across the open lot and even in his direction. Hunkering down in his seat, hoping his baseball cap and sunglasses were enough of a disguise, he watched. She looked so carefree and innocent, but he knew differently. She flaunted herself at him and when he was too weak to resist, she wouldn't give him what he wanted, what they *both* wanted.

Watching the red-haired driver come around the car, take her hand and kiss it, Tyler's hands gripped the steering wheel tighter until he was sure it would snap.

"So, you've whored yourself out already?" he demanded staring at Ness through his windshield. "Well, sweetie, daddy's here and you've been a *very* naughty girl."

Chapter

Ten

Ness stared out across the parking lot seeing the small rustic town. An unseasonably warm seventy degree day with light clouds dotting here and there and a cooling breeze rustling her red hair, Ness looked over at Orin walked up beside her.

"Beautiful, isn't it?" Orin asked.

"Stunning," she agreed. "I could imagine living here. Seeing such beauty every day would be a dream."

"It certainly is that," he replied. "I am glad you are here, Nessa."

"Thank you, Mr. O'Quinn," she said. "I didn't mean to be a bother though."

"It's Orin, love, and you are not a bother," he countered. "Why would you think that?"

She shrugged. "I've been called it before."

"Not by us," Orin said firmly just as Emmet came back from the ticket counter and handed each of them their passes.

Cabhan's children pulled their father to the gift shop, laughing. His kind eyes, aquiline nose, and dimple that was barely covered by days old beard growth, lent him a handsome face.

"Lunch at the Mill in two hours?" Orin called after him.

"I've got my mobile," Cabhan answered before disappearing into the gift shop.

"How long has Cabhan been married?" Ness asked Emmet when he walked up to her.

"Let's see, Lachlan is twelve... and they were married three – two? – years before him," Emmet debated.

"They'll have been married for fifteen years in October," Sean said behind them. "I was ten when they were married. I was the ringbearer."

"I bet you looked adorable in a mini tux," Ness giggled.

"Oh, I took my duties very seriously," Sean grinned.

Ness laughed once more before they started walking to the gate. Orin, Deirdre, and Siobhan headed to the gardens while Ness looked this way and that trying to see the castle.

"We have to get past the entrance gate love, then there's a small path through the grounds and you'll be able to see it," Emmet explained.

"I guess I'm that transparent, huh?" she grinned.

"A little," he chuckled.

Ness caught Sean's laugh as he walked ahead with Keera. Ness was happy to have both Emmet and Sean but she knew she shouldn't be feeling the way she was toward an engaged man. Still, she couldn't deny the chemistry between them, but she could fight it. She may love the feeling of forbidden desire that lingered between them, but she knew she could never allow either of them to act upon it. It wouldn't be fair to Trish. Though, after seeing Trish and Innis kissing on the side of the house, Ness wondered why she worried about Trish's feelings.

"We're almost there," Emmet said and indicated the path before them. "You should be able to see it soon."

As he spoke, they rounded the bend and Ness stopped in her tracks. A little further off, over the tops of the trees, touching the blue sky, loomed the ruins of Blarney Castle. Its towers reached high in an intimidating way, its narrow arrow slits, which served as defense and windows, peppered the imposing stone building. A circular guard tower stood before it and almost as if she were dreaming, she could see how it once was. It was beautiful. Majestic. Mysterious. Inviting.

Emmet walked up beside her and dropped his arm around her shoulders. She jumped and looked over at him. His boyish smirk made her grin stretch from ear to ear.

"This is amazing, Emmet," she said.

"Yeah," he answered. "'Tis. But unfortunately for you, there's no half naked romance novel heroes waiting at the top."

Her gaze turned back to him and she bit her lower lip playfully. "I don't know," she replied eyeing him.

"I know, I know, I'm hot. But contain yourself, woman. Come on," he laughed. "Sean and Keera have already gotten to the bridge."

"There's a draw bridge?" She asked excitedly as they started walking again.

"Eh... no," he answered. "It's just a small, wooden bridge." His words came out in staccato. "There's a small stream and a lot of foliage, so they built a bridge to help everyone walk through."

"Then lead on, Mr. O'Quinn," she grinned. "Let me daydream about my Irish Rogue as I watch you walk ahead."

He threw his head back and laughed. "Get up here, ya," he said.

Pulling her to him, he wrapped an arm around her shoulders. To anyone they passed, it looked like they were a couple, but Ness was glad for his support. She couldn't seem to get Sean out of her head as she thought about her half-naked Irish Rogue on the cover of the romance novel she had read on the plane. And as she stood under the Irish sky, she couldn't help but remember the story in all its fantastic Irish detail. Taking a deep breath, she tried to clear away the desire she felt for him and focus solely on the experiences.

The castle loomed before them and Ness took another moment to take in the sheer beauty of the ancient building. Raising her camera, she took a snapshot of the castle with the sun shining directly into the camera. The castle was cast in shadow. It was an impressive shot and she was giddy wanting to print and frame the picture.

Trying not to look too much like a tourist, Ness quietly asked to take a picture of Keera, Sean, and Emmet. Emmet readily agreed. Grabbing his brother and cousin, and pulling them into his sides, he posed for a photo. Ness snapped a quick picture.

"All right, girl," Emmet held out his hand for her camera. "Your turn."

She nearly giggled. Posing at the bridge, she waited for Emmet to snap a picture of her.

"Sean," Emmet called to brother as a mischievous

smile crossed his lips.

"What do you think they're talking about?" Ness asked Keera as she watched Sean shake his head adamantly at something Emmet had said.

Her best friend shrugged but frowned heavily at her phone, then huffed.

"No clue," she spat. "Who knows what goes through those men's minds?"

"Everything all right?" Ness asked.

"Fine," she answered putting her phone in her back pocket. "Why wouldn't it be? Men are such necessary evils."

Ness laughed in agreement. Finally, she saw Sean sigh harshly but nod at Emmet. Walking back over to Ness, Sean looked down.

"So, ehm, Emmet has thought of a picture he'd like to take of us," Sean said.

"Oh," Ness replied. "Okay."

"Listen to the whole story before you agree, Ness. It's not what you might think." Sean sighed. "He wants us to pose as a couple on the cover of a romance novel."

Ness's jaw dropped as she gaped at him. "You can't be serious."

"He says he won't give you back your camera until you do, and he will tell Trish certain things I don't really want her to know about me as a boy, if I don't," Sean said.

"I can't do that! Is he blackmailing us?" she replied shocked.

"Sounds like it," Sean answered.

Keera laughed beside them. "Oh, come on, Ness,

you're always reading those books with that type of cover pic. Make one of your own."

"I can't!" she exclaimed. "At least not with *you*!" She looked desperately at Sean.

"Listen, I don't want it any more than you do," Sean replied. "But let's just do it and get it over with."

"Real romantic, Sean," Keera rolled her eyes.

"Get out of the shot, Kee," Emmet called, and Keera stepped back.

"Oh god, I'm sorry. Fine," Ness finally agreed. "How do you want it, Emmet?"

"Well considering Sean can't take his shirt off without drawing attention to himself," Emmet said. "Not that he ever minds it."

"Shut it," Sean called back.

Emmet chuckled. "How about this?"

Emmet posed them both; Sean turned with his back to the camera and Ness stood beside him, facing Emmet. Her eyes were visible over Sean's shoulder. Emmet had Sean wrap his arm around Ness's waist and placed Ness's hand on his upper arm. Sean's face was turned to look at her profile. Her other hand was around the back of Sean's head and in his cropped hair.

Emmet stepped back and called out to his brother, "Hold her closer."

Sean winced but tightened his grip around her. Ness gasped when their bodies pressed flush to each other's. Sean looked down at her and for a moment the world stopped spinning and it was just them. The wind caught Ness's hair and it covered her face. With his free hand, Sean pushed her bangs out of her eyes. Ness's breath caught.

Forbidden Desire rang in her ears. She knew it was wrong. Not only was he engaged, she hardly knew him. But none of that mattered when she felt his subtle breath on her face. She swallowed and unconsciously licked her lips.

"Well, I think that's a wrap," Emmet's voice behind him made them jump. Ness pulled away quickly but not before she heard Sean curse silently.

"Was it good for you?" Sean asked Emmet sarcastically.

"Incredibly so," Emmet grinned. "Come on, Ness. You've got to see the grand event. You going to kiss it?"

"Uh... Kiss what?" Ness asked, her head still whirling from being in Sean's arms.

"The Stone," Emmet smirked. "What did you think I meant?"

"I didn't know what you meant, Emmet," she replied sweetly. "You always have the most random thoughts."

"That's me," he laughed. "Come on."

"I've seen it and kissed it. I'm gonna find Ma," Keera said looking down at her phone. "You good?"

"Totally," Ness replied and watched Keera walk towards the gardens.

Following Emmet up the walkway and steps to the entrance of the castle, they stopped in different rooms and read plaques about what occurred there. Eventually, they entered the main part of the castle and Emmet turned to her.

"Are you afraid of heights?" he asked. She shook her head. "Good, what about tight spaces?" He asked.

"How tight?"

"Pretty tight."

"I'm not too good with tight spaces," she admitted.

"I'll go first, Sean will be right behind you. If you need either of us, we'll be there," he said. "Won't we?" he looked toward his brother.

Sean nodded. After Emmet went on ahead to the small doorway, Ness looked back at Sean.

"It's all right," Sean said. "I'll be right here, no matter what." She smiled and nodded. "I am glad you and Emmet are friends."

"He's really sweet," she replied. Emboldened, perhaps by her surroundings or maybe the intimate touch they experienced posing for the picture, she reached out and laid her palm flush against his chest. She felt his heartbeat quicken beneath her fingers. "I like you more," she whispered.

"I'm glad," he choked.

"I wish things could be different."

"So do I."

"You will make an amazing husband to Trish. I only wish I was as fortunate as she is," she went on.

"Perhaps you will be, one day," he replied.

Her hand slid up to his neck then cupped his jaw, her middle finger massaging that small indention behind his earlobe.

"I don't deserve a happily ever after," she whispered.

"Everyone does," he said.

She shook her head and locked eyes with him. "Even murderers?"

Sean's brows furrowed. "Murder? Or self-defense?"

She closed her eyes. "I told you to stay away from me, Sean," she said. "I'm serious when I say I'm dangerous."

"And I'm serious when I tell you I'm not going anywhere, so you can stop trying to scare me off," he replied.

"You're a good man, Sean," she said. "I would have enjoyed an opportunity to get to know you."

"Don't shut me out, Nessa," he breathed.

"I have to."

"Why?"

"For your own protection… and mine," she replied.

"Ness?" Emmet called from the stairs.

She turned and held up a hand asking for a moment.

"Please, Sean, stay away," she begged before dropping her hand and turning away from him. Walking to the steps, she followed Emmet up the winding stone staircase and didn't look back.

Chapter

Eleven

Deirdre, Siobhan, and Keera walked together toward the gardens while Orin hung back checking something on his phone. The women were laughing and teasing each other but Orin had just received a reply from his friend Daniel with the NYPD.

"Dee, Siobh, Keera," he called. They turned to him. Motioning to a small alcove where they would not be noticed, he spoke again. "Loves, I got a reply from Daniel in New York about Ness."

"And?" Deirdre asked.

"It's what Ness said but she left out the part that her hospital records dating back to when she was sixteen were filled with broken bones, bruises, and sprains. When the police questioned her about her stepfather's shooting, she had a fading bruise on her cheek and wouldn't look them in the eye," Orin explained.

"I remember that," Keera said. "She first told me tripped and stumbled into a doorframe. I didn't believe her. She told the cops something different."

"Aye, love. It looks like her mother filed charges against her stating Ness had pulled the trigger, but she was not home at the time, so her witness testimony was inadmissible. Ness's story was that she had been home when her stepfather came home, drunk. He had hit her and tried to force himself on her, the bastard. But she got away and said everything after that was a blur. She remembered someone broke into the house and shot him, but she ran out the back and the police took several days to track her down. The magistrate, the D.A. did not file charges against her due to the police accepting that version of events."

"But he didn't die," Siobhan spat. "The bastard that tried to rape her."

Orin locked eyes with his sister. "No, he didn't," he answered. "Everyone thought he would after two in the chest, but he pulled through the surgery and disappeared. There are still a few warrants out on him. Disorderly Conduct, Public Indecency, Public Intoxication, and Assault. Daniel says in his email that he was able to contact the detective in charge back he's retired since and he actually lives here in Ireland now, County Clare. Jonathan Greene is his name and he said that Ness had left to go to college and then to Ireland before Tyler, the stepfather, disappeared. The Detective was glad to have news of her and asked us to warn her. She does not know that he is still alive."

"Orin, you don't think," Deirdre breathed.

"It is possible, love," he answered.

"What?" Keera looked from one to the other.

"It is possible her stepfather is here in Ireland," Orin replied.

Emmet was right about tight spaces. The stairs going up to the Blarney Stone were narrow, slippery, and there was only a thick rope hanging down the center to hold on to. Ness nearly went down on her hands and knees to crawl up the steps, but with Emmet in front of her and Sean behind her, she felt safe.

Ness's legs began to shake with exertion and adrenaline as she continued to climb.

"Almost there," Sean's voice came from behind her. She took a deep breath and nodded.

They passed empty room after empty room. Some were in ruins and barred so no one could enter, others were open, and she saw tourists milling about taking pictures. As she passed one room, she saw a face she recognized. Before she could think, she screeched and did a double take, nearly tripping Sean as he headed up behind her.

"What's wrong?" Emmet came back down a couple steps. Luckily, there was no one behind them.

Ness looked frantically in the room and saw a man standing a little farther away from everyone.

"That's not possible." She would know him anywhere. "You can't be here!" She shouted, stepping out of the stairwell and into the room. "There's no way you can possibly be here! Do you hear me? You can't hurt me ever again!" The man finally turned around and she froze. It wasn't Tyler.

Sean was by her side in an instant. "Ness?" He questioned softly.

"I'm sorry," she said to the man. "I thought you were someone else."

"No worries, my dear," the man smiled. "I'm glad I'm not."

Emmet came around and, as Sean helped Ness to a corner, apologized to the older man again. Thankfully, he just waved them off with a smile and a leprechaun-like wink. Emmet walked over to his brother and Ness.

"I'm sorry," Ness said to them.

"It's all right," Sean replied. "What happened?"

"It's nothing," she crossed her arms over her chest.

"Ness, you nearly attacked that man thinking he was someone else," Emmet summarized. "We're you're friends. We care about you. Let us help. You do not have to fight this alone anymore. Tell us what's going on."

She took a deep breath and looked over at Sean who smiled and nodded his encouragement.

"I... I thought he was my stepdad," she admitted.

"I thought he was shot," Emmet offered.

She nodded. "Tyler was a nasty man," she continued. Sean stiffened. "He used to hit me." Anger simmered just below Sean's and Emmet's cool exterior. "When my mom wasn't home, he would get really drunk... I mean *really* drunk and he would get angry for the littlest thing. I would have a black eye before I knew what was going on. Eventually, I locked myself in my room when I knew I would be alone with him. But it didn't matter, he would just kick the door down. If you look into my ER history, you'd see a few broken bones along with the black eyes and bruises. I've never told anyone about this." She looked at them. Sean's face contorted in anger and Emmet's eyes blazed. "I don't know why I'm telling you this."

"You said he couldn't be here," Emmet started. "Why?"

"He's dead," she said simply. Sean and Emmet said nothing, prompting her to continue. "He can't be here."

"Ness, I'm sorry, but Keera found this on the floor of your room. It was buzzing. She gave it to me to look after," Sean said producing her cell phone. She looked at it for a moment then her eyes snapped up to his.

"Did you go through my text messages?" She demanded.

"I'm sorry but there were some pretty sick things and I needed to know what was going on," Sean explained.

"How dare you," she breathed. "Keera did this?"

"We're both genuinely worried about you," Sean replied. "I know it was wrong, but we want to help."

"I can take care of myself," she barked.

"Ness," Emmet placed a hand on her shoulder. Her burning eyes turned to him as she shrugged him off. "Listen, I know what Sean did and keeping it from you seems like a stupid thing to do, but trust me, love, whatever he did, he did out of concern for you. Sean cares for you as I do. We want to protect you, if we can. Let us."

"He shouldn't have looked through my private things," she said.

"Agreed and I believe he's heartily sorry for doing that," Emmet said looking over at his brother. "But it couldn't be helped. Trust us, Ness. We would do nothing to harm you. We want to help you."

She looked from one to the other of them. Finally, she nodded and stood. Placing her arms around them, she hugged as tightly as she could.

"Thank you for worrying about me, it's a new thing for me," she said. "I'm not used to it. Just promise me you'll not keep something like that from me and I'll try and let you in to help me."

"Agreed," Emmet smiled. "Now, let's finish what we came here for. You're going to have to kiss the Blarney before someone kisses you first," he winked at his brother.

"Will you trust two quirky Irishmen to see you safely to the top?" Sean asked, taking Ness's hand and holding it gently.

She giggled slightly, happy for the release of tension. "Not so sure about quirky. How about roguishly handsome?"

Emmet smirked and Sean chuckled.

"Well, now, I do like the sound of that," Emmet said offering her his arm.

Chapter

Twelve

The view from the top of the battlements was worth any claustrophobia Ness experienced on the stairs. She could see for miles around. On one side, landscape as green as green could be with a row of trees cutting through the middle of the field. On the other, a view of the town just outside the grounds.

Since the walkway was too narrow for more than two people to walk across, Sean and Emmet trailed behind her. Ness snapped picture after picture all along the battlements.

Surprisingly with the amount of people around her, it was extremely quiet. She didn't know if the wind was carrying the voices and conversations away from her or if everyone was as mesmerized as she was. Whatever it was, the landscape took her breath away. Turning back to Sean and Emmet with the biggest grin she'd ever had, she snapped a candid photo of them.

After a beat, Sean indicated the end of the walkway where a large camera was stationed. "You going to kiss the stone?"

"Ooh," she breathed. "I've come this far. How bad could it be?"

Sean and Emmet exchanged looks and chuckled. She knew then kissing the Blarney Stone wasn't going to be as easy as she had thought.

"What excuse can we come up with this time?" Trish asked as she stroked the fine hairs on Innis's chest. Taking a deep breath, he held her closer to him.

"Stress?" he offered, kissing the top of her hair. No matter how many times he thought his lust was satisfied, every time she looked at him or touched him, he felt as if it was the first time.

He refused to think the reason he needed her that day was because of the kiss she shared with his brother. Innis refused to admit he was selfish and jealous. He was never a jealous lover, but seeing them kiss, though he had seen it many times before, was the last straw. Holding her closer, the thought of standing beside his brother as she pledged to love, honor, and obey him, was abhorrent.

She stiffened in his arms, then sat up suddenly. "Oh Jaysus, what was I thinking?"

"Hey, it's all right," he said leaning up beside her and trailing his fingers down her back.

"How is this all right?" She demanded clutching the sheets around her chest and turning scathing eyes on him.

"He doesn't need to know."

"He never will," she swore. "You *can't* tell him."

Reaching up, he buried his fingers in her hair. "I would never do that to you," he said.

She softened and nuzzled his hand, covering it with hers.

"I like you – this – us, far too much, Innis," she said and his heart soared.

Plowing ahead, he spoke, "if I were to ask you to leave him and come away with me… What would you say?"

"I would say you're still high from shagging," she said. "You're daft if you think I'd do that!"

"He will never love you the way I do," he replied.

"What?"

He had not intended for that to slip out.

"Brilliant, bloody brilliant," she nearly shouted gathering the sheets around her and standing from the bed.

"Trish," he tried. "I just… I can't stop thinking about you, about us."

"How many times?" she shouted. "There is no *us!*" Stalking to the bathroom she slammed door.

Flopping back down on the bed, Innis covered his face with his forearm. Whenever he was around her, let alone whenever he slept with her, he couldn't think straight. One thing was certain, he couldn't stand by as she married his little brother. He would never be able to sit at the dinner table across from her without thinking of their times together. He would never be able to forget the way she molded to him. The way she responded to him. The absolute ecstasy he felt in her arms. Sean couldn't have her.

Chapter

Thirteen

Kissing the stone had to have been one of the scariest things Ness had seen in her life. She watched other tourists sit down and bend over backwards, reach over their heads, and grab on to the iron bars bolted to the stone of the wall. The Castle worker beside them, held on to their hips and eased them further down. It was thrilling in its danger and Ness was up next.

The worker looked up at her and smiled. "Come on then. Sit ya bum down on the blanket here." He indicated the place beside him. "I've got ya. You can't fall. Promise. Besides there's iron rods beneath." Ness peered down the large hole to see the iron rods preventing anyone from falling to the ground below.

Looking back at Sean and Emmet, they nodded and coaxed her on. Sitting down beside the worker, she scooted to the edge of the stone floor. "Now, you see the smooth stone at the base of the wall there?" the worker asked. She nodded. "That's the one to kiss."

"That's pretty far down," she replied.

"You can do it," Sean promised.

"Here goes."

The worker took hold of her hips as she bent backwards and took hold of the iron bars behind her. The worker helped ease her down until she was at eye level with the stone. Leaning forward, she kissed it.

"Well done," the worker cheered and raised her back up.

A sense of accomplishment flooded through her. She couldn't help the smile that was as big as her face. Emmet and Sean cheered.

"Have you guys ever done that?" She asked.

"Oh yeah," Sean drolled.

"We were but wee lads at the time, though," Emmet smiled.

Walking further around the rectangle of the battlements, Sean's hand kept bumping into hers. Throwing caution to the wind, Ness grasped his hand in hers. Startled, he gazed down at their intertwined fingers then looked back up at her.

"Okay?" she questioned. He nodded. "I'm not trying to cause a problem. I'm not some home wrecker."

"I know that."

They stayed quiet until they reached the other side of the castle battlements, Ness looked out at the different view.

"What is that?" she asked seeing a stunning stately

manor home a stone's throw from the castle.

"That's Blarney House," Emmet explained. "It's the ancestral seat of the MacCarthy's. It's still a working home but they allow tours. It's quite lovely."

"You're a walking Irish encyclopedia, Em," Sean teased. Emmet laughed.

"It's stunning," Ness replied.

"Would you like to go see it?" Sean asked.

"Do we have time?"

"We have no schedule," Sean answered.

She grinned at him and squeezed his hand. "I really would."

"Good," he said. "Let's go and see your pictures first. You might want a souvenir of your first Irish experience."

"Pictures?" she questioned.

"It's like a roller-coaster ride," Emmet explained holding up a ticket stub. "That's why the big camera."

"Oh no," she replied holding her hair out of her face as a gust of wind blew it. "I didn't know they would take my picture."

"It's too late now, love," Emmet teased.

"Come on," Sean said.

"Wait, could I have a picture of you two?" she asked.

Standing near a cutout in the wall, Sean and Emmet stood on either side, Blarney House between them in the distance. Ness backed up as far as she could. Her back rested on the iron railing of the walkway. Leaning back just enough to snap the picture, Ness lined up the viewfinder and took two pictures. Lowering the camera, her smile faded when she saw Emmet staring just over her shoulder.

"Are you okay?" she asked him. Emmet jerked back.

"Yeah," he forced a smile. "Go on down. I'll be right behind you."

"What's wrong?" she asked starting to turn around. Emmet caught her wrist gently.

"Nothing," he replied smiling. "Go on. I'll be right there."

Sean took her arm and walked towards the exit. Once they were in the courtyard again, Ness turned to look at him.

"Do you think Emmet is okay?" she asked.

"No clue, but I'm sure he's fine," Sean replied. "Come on, there's the gift shop."

Walking with him to the small gift shop built at the base of the castle, she handed the attendant the ticket and they posted her pictures on the screen.

"I don't normally do this. I've never bought a picture from an amusement park, but this is different," she explained indicating to the salesperson she wanted to purchase both pictures.

"Anything else? They have some pretty neat souvenirs," Sean said.

She looked around and picked a few items, handing them to the girl behind the counter. When she rang up the items, Sean pulled out his wallet.

"Oh, no," Ness said looking over at him. "I was going to get it."

"I know you were," he grinned. "But I want to. Let me."

She decided it would be easier if she didn't argue but

her stomach was knotting. She was serious when she said she was no home wrecker but she was starting to feel like one.

"Thanks," she tried to smile.

"You're welcome," he answered. "It's my pleasure. Enjoy," he handed the bag to Ness.

"Thanks again," she said. Before Sean could say anything, else Emmet appeared at the stairwell exit, a fierce expression on his face.

"Em," Sean waved him over. Emmet's eyes were burning, his lip was split, and a small drop of blood oozed out of the crack. "What the bloody hell happened to you?"

"Nothing," Emmet said tightly. "Let's go." He grabbed Ness's elbow a little too harshly and pulled her away.

"Emmet, you're hurting me," she said. "What happened?"

"I said it was nothing, now let's go," he ordered.

"Emmet," Sean rebuked.

Ness yanked her arm out of his grasp and stopped. "No. It's clearly not *nothing*, now what happened?"

Emmet's jaw muscles flexed. Taking a deep breath, he locked eyes with her.

"A man was watching you," he admitted. "And me, us... I didn't like his look. I waited in one of the rooms and pulled him inside. I demanded to know why he was watching us. Without warning, he threw a punch. Split my lip. We wrestled. Finally, another couple lads split us up. By the time I shrugged them off, the man was gone. Now will you listen to me? Let's go."

"What did this guy look like?" she asked.

"What? You want his shoe size? How the hell do I

know? I saw his fist," Emmet replied heatedly.

"Emmet," her voice was devoid of emotion.

Sighing, he went on, "about five ten. He was wearing a hat, jeans, and a sweater. He was an evil looking bugger."

"Did he have a scar on his cheek?" she asked calmly.

"Yeah," Emmet replied. "In the shape of a hook, why?"

Without warning, her knees gave out and she collapsed into Sean's arms.

Chapter

Fourteen

"*Nessa!*" *he screamed. He was always screaming when he was drunk. "You let me in this minute, do you hear me?!"*

Ness's cheek throbbed from where the back of his hand had collided with it five minutes ago. She didn't cry. He always said he liked it when she cried. Ever since the day she turned sixteen after her mom had married him, she had not shed one tear.

"Unlock this damn door!" He shouted. Then, to her horror, the door rattled.

Diving for her nightstand, she felt around for the cold steel. Her fingers found the grip just as the door caved in.

Screaming.

Point... Shoot...

"Ness, can you hear me?" a voice called through the darkness.

"Is she gonna be all right, da'?" another younger voice asked panicked.

"Ness," the first voice called. "Can you open your eyes?"

Slowly, her eyes opened and she stared into two toffee colored irises. Cabhan stood over her.

"Do you know where you are?" he asked softly.

She slowly became aware she was on the ground resting comfortably in someone's arms. Turning, she saw Sean holding her to him, his own toffee colored eyes reflecting worry. Emmet stood beside Sean. Cabhan's children flanked their father.

"How do you feel?" Cabhan took something that looked like a pill from Sean. She felt the burn of smelling salts in her nose.

Looking over at Emmet, she saw his swollen and bloodied lip and everything she thought was a dream, came back to her. "He's here. He can't be here!" She cried.

"What are you saying?" Sean asked.

"My stepfather," she started. "He can't be here!"

"Calm down, Nessa," Cabhan ordered. "Now, can you get up?"

She nodded. Sean supported her as Cabhan took her hands and steadied her.

"Did I really just do that? I've never fainted in my life," she replied dusting herself off.

"You've had a shock." Cabhan turned to his brothers. "She needs to walk around, slowly. Clear her head. Go with her. I'll see if there's a paramedic on site. She should be checked out by someone used to looking after humans."

"Really I'm okay, Cabhan," she called after him. "Thank you."

"You're getting checked out, Ness, that's all that there is to it," he replied in that O'Quinn stubborn voice she was sensing all the O'Quinn lads seemed to have. "Fiona, Lachlan, stay close to your Uncle Emmet and don't wander off."

"We won't, da'," Lachlan promised.

Cabhan nodded and looked once more at Emmet. "You should get that lip checked out too."

"I've had worse, even from you," Emmet waved him off.

Cabhan huffed and put his hands on his hips. "Why did I devote seven years of my life studying medicine if my family doesn't listen to me?"

"Fine, I bow to your extensive medical knowledge, old man," Emmet said. "Call me when you have the paramedic."

"Take care of Lachlan and Fiona," Cabhan said.

"You know I will," Emmet answered.

Once Cabhan left, Sean wrapped an arm around Ness's waist and helped her down the slight incline towards the archway into the courtyard. Out of the walls of the castle and into the grounds, there were several park benches lining a path towards the gardens. After a moment, Ness turned to Emmet and threw her arms around his neck.

"Are you okay?" she mumbled into his shoulder.

"Aye, I'm fine, love," he answered holding her tightly.

"Don't worry about me. It's just a busted lip. Are *you* all right?" She nodded into his neck and placed a gentle kiss just below his jaw.

"Thank you," she whispered.

"Ach, love, ya know I'd do anything for ye, aye?"

Nodded again, she pulled back. "That means a lot."

"Now, go with Sean. I'll be right behind ye, like," Emmet said.

Sean's arm was wrapped securely around her, as they walked through the grounds to a bench near another guard tower.

"Ness," Sean started.

"I know, Sean," she stopped him and sighed. "I'll tell you what you want to know."

"That man Emmet fought with and described to you," he started. "Who is he?"

"It's hard to explain," she began. Breaking away from him, she went to a tree that lined the path and leaned against it. "The man he described cannot be here."

"Why? Who is he?" Sean asked not moving.

She wrapped her arms around herself warding off the fear as she told him her most deadly secret. "My stepfather," she replied.

"But," Sean's brows furrowed. "You said your stepfather is dead."

"He is..." she replied. "I shot him."

Chapter

Fifteen

Sean couldn't say he was surprised. Though Ness had always tried to hide her past, her talk of how she was dangerous, or how murderers don't get a happily ever after paved the groundwork. Her confession, though serious, proved to Sean she was strong, capable, but scared.

"It's okay," Ness finally went on. "I understand what you must think of me. But please, hear the whole story before you judge me."

Sean took a step toward her. Turning her to face him, he gently lifted her chin with his fingers and gazed into her emerald green eyes.

"Whatever happened," he started. "You cannot be blamed. You must have had a reason. You do not have to tell me anything you don't want to. I just want to help you. I know you have secrets, we all do. It's all right. You hardly know me and I'm not free to help you the way I want. But whatever happened, know I would never judge you."

Ness took a deep shaky breath. "He tried to rape me."

Sean's eyes widened but he said nothing.

Ness sat on the park bench behind her. "I'm adopted you see. I've never known my birth parents. The couple who adopted me was amazing. But when my dad died, I was fourteen and my mom couldn't support us alone. When I turned sixteen, she remarried. Tyler preyed on her insecurities. He was sophisticated in a Dracula sense. Cunning and manipulative. Mom thought he would be a great role model for me. He proclaimed to be a successful businessman, but he was actually a professional gambler, and he wasn't any good at it. She took two jobs just so we were not evicted. He lived with us for two years. Drunk and abusive to my mom. Once, I witnessed him hit her after that I stepped in the way. That's when he got a taste for hitting me. Mom would work a lot of nights and he would come home drunk. I knew it wouldn't be long before he tried to… take advantage of me," she looked down.

"I started locking myself in my room whenever I was alone with him. One night he came home earlier than I expected, and I ran to my room, but he caught me and tried to kiss me. I struggled and he hit me. Picking me up, he tried to kiss me," she shivered. "I still remember the disgusting taste of his lips soaked in cheap bourbon, nacho cheese, and cigarettes. It made me want to vomit. I kicked him between the legs and ran to my room, locking the door. When he followed me, he tried to break my door down. I was panicked. My grandfather, my adopted dad's father, was an old army guy and he gave me his army pistol before he died. When Tyler hit me the first time, I found took it from the safe and hid it in my room. Even drunk Tyler was strong.

"When he broke down the door, I didn't think, I just pulled the trigger. Twice. The bullets struck him in the chest, and he fell back against the opposite wall. Mom walked in the door and ran to him. She screamed at me to call an ambulance but when I refused, and she saw the gun in my hand, she swore she would see me in jail for daring to hurt him. She had this twisted need for him. I dropped the gun and ran. I haven't stopped running. Eventually the police caught up with me at college. Keera was there. She knows most of this but not that I shot him. I told the cops there was an intruder and he shot him. But I don't think they believed me.

"The police didn't press charges and Keera told me about Ireland and a way to start again. I knew my birth parents were from here and the detective in charge mentioned in passing that Ireland is a haven. I think he knew the truth. I thought I could put it all behind me. But somehow, he's alive and well and followed me here. He will never stop. He wants me and now he'll make me pay. He must've thought Emmet was my boyfriend or something. I don't know. Maybe that's why he attacked him. He sent me texts telling me he was following me as you saw.

"I need to go. I can leave and start again somewhere else. I can't drag you all into this. I can't burden anyone else with the truth. You have every right to turn me over to the police, but I hope you won't. Let me just go away. Disappear. I'm good at that."

The second she looked up at him, Sean framed her face and captured her lips with his. It was a strong, possessing kiss. A kiss to tell her he was still there. At first, he could sense her surprise but soon she wrapped her hand behind his neck and returned his kiss. He held her close to him as his hands explored her hair. Their lips moved together fitting together like they were meant to be. She was tentative in her movements and it made him wonder if she was new to kissing.

When he eventually pulled away, she shivered. Looking into her glazed eyes, he saw a look of pure innocence and affection. He playfully nipped at her nose and kissed the wetness away from her cheeks.

"Never run away from me," he pleaded. "I'll never be able to let you go."

"But you're getting married," she reasoned.

"I don't know what to do yet," he said honestly. "I don't feel for her what I feel for you. Yes, Trish and I are friends, yes, we've been together for a long time, but I've never had a kiss like that."

"Was it good?" she asked.

"Very."

"Good, I wanted to know if I kissed well. It was my first time," she confided.

The fiery flash of possession tore through him and his lips twisted in a roguish smirk. "Did you enjoy it?"

"Very much."

"Good," he whispered. She giggled but then looked away.

"We can't do that again."

"I know, not yet anyway," he said.

"I'm not going to break you and your fiancée up, Sean. I'm not like that. We need to stay away from each other."

"Until I figure out what to do, I agree."

"But it has to be your decision. I can't ask you to do anything. I don't ask you to do anything."

"I know, love," he answered. "But right now, I can see Emmet, Lachlan, and Fiona heading our way."

They separated quickly as Emmet walked up.

"Cabhan's on his way. I told him where we are."

"Good," Sean answered. He looked back at Ness and asked. "Are you hungry?"

"Starving, honestly," she replied.

"We'll meet ma and da' at the Mill after you both are looked at by the paramedic," Sean said. "It's a great place for food and a drink, and from the looks of you two, you could use one, or maybe two."

"Uncle Sean," ten-year-old Fiona piped up. Sean pulled her onto his lap and gave her a squeeze.

"What is it, love?" he asked.

"Why were you kissing Miss Nessa when you're marrying Auntie Trish?" She asked.

A knot grew in the pit of his stomach. No one was supposed to have seen their kiss. If Fiona had seen them, Trish would find out quicker than a wildfire on dried heather. He gulped and looked up at Emmet. Luckily before anyone could answer, Cabhan walked up with a medic beside him.

Tyler watched from the battlements. His plan was working better than he ever thought possible. Rubbing his sore ribs where the mammoth of a man barreled into him, he smirked. If the guy wasn't her boyfriend, he at least cared about her more than any generic acquaintance.

"After I'm done with Ness, you're next, *laddie*," he sneered.

Chapter

Sixteen

After Emmet and Ness were checked by the paramedic, Cabhan turned to his brothers.

"Now would anyone care to tell me what the hell is going on here?" he demanded.

"Ooh, Dadai," Fiona sing-songed. "I'm telling Mamai you cursed in front of us."

Cabhan sighed harshly. "Would someone *kindly* tell me what's going on?" he asked as a show.

"Oh, I know! I know!" Fiona jumped up and down. "Uncle Sean was kissing Miss Nessa!"

Cabhan's eyes flew to his brother's. "What?"

"It's not what you think," Sean replied.

"Cabhan, I'm sorry," Ness started. "I'm petrified of

heights and didn't tell anyone. Once I got down on level ground I passed out. Foolish, I know, but it's true."

"I'm not an eejit," Cabhan replied. "You being afraid of heights doesn't account for Emmet's busted lip. Now, why don't you tell me what *really* happened?"

"Will it suffice to say this girl is under our protection?" Emmet spoke up. "If you need to know any more, I will be the first one to tell you, with Ness's permission."

"No, Emmet it's not enough," Cabhan stated. "My children's safety is at stake here. I'll not have them put in harm's way. So, either you tell me what is going on right now, or I'm taking this to the Garda."

Ness took a deep breath as Emmet and Sean jumped to her defense against Cabhan. Ness never dropped the eldest O'Quinn's gaze.

"Cabhan," Ness finally said softly, causing the others to stop talking over each other. "I will tell you everything. But for your children's sake only." She turned to Sean. "Emmet needs to know too."

"I'm not leaving," Sean said.

"I don't want the children to hear."

"Ness, I'm not leaving you," Sean replied.

"Oh, saints!" Cabhan was exasperated. "Fine! Just tell me this. Are my children safe?"

"As far as I know, yes," she answered. "It's me he wants."

"Who?" he asked. "You know what? Never mind. This whole bloody business is annoying."

"Da'," his son pressed when Cabhan let another curse slip.

Cabhan sighed harshly. "As soon as my children are safely with their mother, I want to know what is going on."

"Okay, you deserve no less than the truth," she agreed.

"Good," Cabhan replied. "Lachlan, Fiona, your grandparents are waiting for us for lunch. We'll be at the Mill," he said to his brothers as he steered his children back toward the main path.

"He needs to know," Ness looked over at Emmet.

"I know," Emmet replied.

"So do you," she said.

"I wasn't going to leave you," Sean piped up.

"I would have been here, Sean," Emmet stated.

"Aye," Sean answered. "But, I've heard her story and I'm not letting her out of my sight," he turned to Ness. "You're not running anymore."

Ness stared at him for a long moment, then Emmet cleared his throat.

"You know, we all saw you two," Emmet said. "I don't mean to make things awkward, but Sean you *are* getting married in a week."

"I know," Sean sighed.

"Perhaps, if we keep our distance for a while, no one will suspect. I am so sorry to have caused this."

"It's on me, love," Sean replied. "I will have to tell Trish before Fiona lets it slip."

She nodded then turned to Emmet. "Would you walk with me to lunch, please? I'm starving."

"My pleasure," Emmet replied.

They started following the path Cabhan had just taken. Ness stopped and looked back at Sean.

"Thank you, for not judging me," she said.

"How could I? You did nothing wrong," Sean answered.

Emmet said nothing beside her but once they were closer to the main entrance, he stopped.

"Did you want to see Blarney House?" he asked.

"After the excitement today, I kinda just want to have lunch and move on," she replied.

"Well, this won't be your last trip here," Emmet winked. She smiled despondently. "Hey, listen, I don't know who that guy was or what happened between the two of you, but I want you to know he's not getting anywhere near you."

"He's no one, Emmet," she squeezed his arm. "He's supposed to be dead. A ghost. He can't hurt me anymore. I won't let him."

"Did he hurt you before?" Emmet asked gently.

"Many times."

Emmet's hand clenched into a fist. "Is he that bastard who hurt you? Your stepfather?" Emmet demanded.

"Yes," she answered.

Emmet said nothing but she saw his thumb go to his lip and wipe some blood off the cut. His eyes were hooded with suppressed anger. "I wish I had hit him harder then."

"Can I ask you something?" she questioned.

"Anything," he answered.

"Why are you so willing to help me?" she asked. "You don't know anything about me."

Emmet smiled slightly. "Because I care about you."

"But you don't know me."

"So?" he asked. Then, as if the conversation was over, he turned back to the walkway, and froze.

"Ah, shite," he breathed. Ness followed his gaze. A woman about six months pregnant was walking with a man and two other children.

"Emmet?" Ness asked. "Who is it?"

"My ex," he sighed.

Her eyes flew to the woman she had heard him mention on their walk earlier that day.

"I didn't ask before but how long has it been?" she asked.

"About ten years."

Ness's eyes went to the eldest child walking beside his mother. He looked nearly ten.

"I know what you're thinking, and the answer is no. He's not mine. He's tall of his age. He's only seven," Emmet explained.

Ness slipped her hand into his. He looked down at the touch then back into her eyes.

"Well, then, how do you want to play this? I'm a pretty good actress," she grinned. He chuckled.

"Like one of your romance novels?" He asked.

"Works for me," she replied leaning into him and placing a kiss on his cheek. He smiled and raised her hand to his lips. They walked on.

"Emmet?" his ex's voice called.

He turned and tucked Ness into his side, playing along.

"Chloe," he nodded. "It's been a while."

"Yeah, it has," she smiled. "At least nine years."

"Ten," he answered then looked at her husband. "Tom."

"Emmet," Tom answered tightly.

"You look well," Emmet said. Tom did not acknowledge the compliment. "When's the wee one due?"

"Sometime in September," Chloe explained.

"Congratulations," Emmet replied. Ness gripped Emmet's arm a little tighter. "Oh, sorry, Ness this is Chloe and Tom. Tom and I were roommates at University. Chloe and I dated for four years."

"Five," she corrected.

"Five," he acquiesced. "This is Ness."

"It's nice to meet you. Em's told me about you. It's good to meet some of his friends from college," Ness said.

"Yeah, you too. We should get going," Tom said guiding his wife around them without another word.

Emmet stood there for a moment and closed his eyes. He took a deep breath and let it out in a huff.

"She's lovely," Ness replied. "And she's still in love with you."

"Yeah," he sighed. "It's not one sided either."

"I can tell," she answered. "Why did she marry your best friend?"

"*Former* best friend," he stressed. "He was the one she

ran to whenever we had a fight and I guess they fell in love."

"Well, he's not nearly as good looking as you are," she replied. When he didn't answer, she rubbed his arm. "Come on, I'm starving."

"And I could use a whiskey," he grumbled.

"So could I," she replied.

"That's it, lass, embrace your Irish roots," he chuckled breaking the tension and draping his arm around her shoulders.

"I hope I am Irish, Emmet," she replied. "But just because my birthparents were here for a time, it doesn't mean they were born here."

"You're Irish, love," he said. "I can feel it."

"It's nice to belong somewhere," she replied.

He tightened his arm around her. "You're always welcome wherever I am. You know, I have a little sister but I kinda like you more."

She bumped him playfully. "I'm glad I was here for you."

"Me too," Emmet smiled.

Chapter

Seventeen

"Trish, come on, love, don't be mad at me," Innis said walking into the kitchen to see Trisha standing over the stove. "I'm an eejit, you know that. When I'm around you I can't think. I'm sorry." He stepped up behind her and wrapped his arms around her. She shrugged out of his embrace.

"I made a mistake sleeping with you, Innis," she said. "Sean thinks I've never been with anyone and that's how I want it. He can never know about us."

"He doesn't know about the other two guys you told me about?" he asked.

She whirled around with a spatula in her hand ready to smack him. He reached up to block her strike.

"I told you that in confidence, thinking you were drunk," she replied.

"The only thing I was drunk on that night was you," he replied. "Does it really matter to him?"

"Yes."

"Why?"

"Because he's never been with anyone," she revealed.

"What?" he breathed. So his baby brother was a virgin, not a big deal, but Innis was surprised he didn't know. Sean teased and taunted as if he had firsthand knowledge. Then after a moment, his eyes narrowed. "You're founding your marriage on a lie."

"I'll tell him eventually but not now."

"You're lying to him."

"It's none of your business why I do what I do with my fiancé," she said.

"Wrong," Innis spat. "He's my brother."

"And you slept with your brother's fiancée," she answered. "Are you going to tell him?"

He was trapped. He knew he should tell Sean. No matter how much he wanted Trish, he could never lose his brother.

"God, I'm an eejit," he breathed thrusting his hands through his hair.

"Stay out of it, Innis," she ordered.

"Do you love him?"

"Does it matter?" she questioned.

"It matters, you're getting married."

"I care about him. We're best friends."

"If you weren't marrying him, would you tell him

about me?"

She huffed. "Leave it, Innis."

"Tell me you don't love me," he said.

"What?" She turned back to him.

"Tell me you don't love me, and I'll walk out of here. You and I will never sleep together again," he began. "Don't say it and I will prove to you that you only think of Sean as a friend."

"Fine, I don't love you," she answered not looking at him. He crowded in and waited for her to look up at him.

"Say it again."

"I don't love you," she stated but her voice hitched and her pupils dilated.

He lowered his lips to suck gently on her collarbone.

"You wouldn't dare," she breathed running her fingers through his hair pulling his closer to her.

"I love you," he said. "I love you more than anything."

She gasped as she pulled him from her collar and slammed her lips on his. Dropping the spatula, she wrapped her body around his.

The Mill was an old building near the center of the town. There were shops along the main street and the restaurant was adjacent to the biggest one. Blarney was the quintessential bustling Irish village. The restaurant had a soup deli and made to order station. The bar was located a step up from the main area and tucked behind the small grocery store containing kitchen wares, cookbooks, and dry mixes. Emmet and Sean flanked Ness as she stood in line. The old-fashioned school-pizza smelled divine and her American diet was rearing its head. She ordered two slices of the square cheese with a bottled water. The rest of the family was sitting at a high-top table near the open doors leading to the patio eatery.

"Ness," Emmet called to her before she walked away. "What would you like from the bar?"

"Oh," she replied. "I don't know. I'm not much of a drinker. Whatever you get is fine."

"I'm getting whiskey, love," he cautioned.

"Ah," she bit her lip debating. "Not sure. I like Sean's whiskey."

"I could do whiskey soda for you?" Emmet offered.

"How about a glass of wine?" she asked. "Crisp white."

"Done, I'll bring it to you."

"Thanks, I have some money in my purse," she offered.

"I've got this," Emmet replied.

"You paid for everything, let me do something," she asked.

"Compromise," Sean interjected. "We're heading through Killarney on the way home instead of the Rock of Cashel. You can get the first round at Sheehan's."

"Deal," she grinned.

"Whiskey for me too, Em," Sean said.

"Preference?"

"Whatever you get, cheers," he said.

"Ness," Deirdre waved her over. "Come sit with me,

love." She indicated a seat. "How did you like Blarney?"

"It was the most beautiful sight I've seen in a very long time," Ness confessed.

"Cabhan was telling us that you had a bit of a fainting spell come upon you, like," Orin said. "Are you all right?"

"Oh yes, silly me," she said looking over at Sean. "I think I hit Emmet too. He's got a bloodied lip. But your sons are such gentlemen, they're not telling me the most embarrassing things I'm sure I did."

"Yes," Keera grinned slumped in her chair. "Fiona's been telling us just how *gentlemanly* Sean's been to you."

"Keera," her mother whispered a reproach as Ness went pale and Sean looked down at his food.

"What, Ma?" Keera asked. "We're all thinking it. Sean, none of us like Trish for you and we would stand behind you if you chose to break off the wedding."

"Keera!" Nearly everyone at the table shouted.

If Sean was a cartoon character, steam would have been coming out of his ears. His face turned red and his eyes looked hard at his cousin. His jaw clenched and Ness heard his teeth grate against each other.

"What?" Keera looked innocently around the table. "We all know she's shagging Innis. Why would he want her now?"

Ness jumped as Sean stood so fast, he knocked his chair out from under him.

"I don't know where you heard such a ridiculous lie, but my fiancée is not *shagging* anyone, not even me. Yes, I like Ness, yes, I kissed her, all right. Everyone here already knows, so why should I deny it? I don't frankly care anymore. I've never felt this way before!" Immediately Sean closed his eyes and cursed.

Ness went pale and slumped in her seat. Sean swallowed, cursed again, and turned around. Emmet stood behind him watching everything. Walking over to his brother, Sean grabbed one of the whiskies in Emmet's hand and gulped it down in two swallows. Everyone stared as he walked out of the restaurant.

"Well," Emmet said looking around. "That certainly was entertaining. Your wine, Ness." He handed it to her with a wink. Taking a small sip, she couldn't enjoy the taste. Once Sean disappeared from view, all eyes turned to look at her.

Nothing could calm Sean down. Even the whiskey warming his belly, made him want to vomit. He had seen Trish's and Innis' connection and his suspicion was now voiced. They've been spending a lot of time together, he wanted to dismiss it. Trisha wouldn't have lied to him.

Sean leaned against a large tree and closed his eyes. He was so tired of everything. Maybe he should go to Belfast for a little while. He had friends up there. Postpone the wedding for a few months. Perhaps then, he could get Ness out of his head. If he could put some distance between them, maybe he could get over the incredibly powerful attraction he had for her and come to the realization he and Trish should be together.

But then what if he was wrong? What if he wasn't tied down to Trish? Maybe, just maybe, he would be able to be closer to Ness. Maybe he would be able to show his affection openly. He was no cheater, but over the last couple days he felt more and more like one.

He never wanted to see a look of disappointment on his father's face or know his mother looked down on him from Heaven and disapproved of the man he'd become. He never wanted to cause Deirdre, who was like a mother to him, to be ashamed of him.

Leaning his head back against the tree trunk, his eyes were closed, and the whiskey soured his stomach. For the first time in his life, he realized he wasn't happy with everything being planned out for him. Ever since he had met Trish, every decision he ever made was made, even asking her to marry him was her choice. Had he ever loved her enough to ask her without the pressure of his friends?

"Sean," his father's deep voice said.

Sighing, he slowly opened his eyes. Orin stood, his hands in the pockets of his jeans, his graying auburn hair was cut short and his toffee colored eyes were serious. Orin wasn't quite as tall as Emmet, but he was just as broad and stood a few inches taller that Sean.

"Da'," Sean greeted.

"Walk with me, lad."

Taking a deep breath, Sean nodded and pushed off the tree trunk. He fell into step beside his father.

"Did I ever tell you I was engaged before I married your mother?" Orin asked after a long moment.

"What?" Sean looked over at him surprised.

"Before I met your mother, not Deirdre, Caitlin," he clarified, speaking of Sean's birthmother. "I was engaged to a woman I had been with for about seven years. We were childhood sweethearts. Our parents were best friends, and everyone knew we would get married. Hell, my mother nearly had the whole thing planned by the time we were sixteen. I asked her to marry me during our Christmas recess my first year at University. Our parents couldn't be happier, but... as much as I cared for her, I looked at her more like a sister than a lover. I would lay awake at night trying to imagine her next to me, carrying my children." He shook his head.

"When we started spring session," he went on. "There was a transfer student from Galway by the name of Caitlin O'Neil," his father broke off with a chuckle. A reminiscent smile crossed Orin's lips. "I still remember when I first saw her. It felt like the world had stopped spinning. Lightning, as I call it. I've said it before, and I'll say it again.

"She sat beside me that first day. We got to know each other, and it got to the point where I couldn't wait to see her. I would dream about her at night and wait for her during the day. I felt like the worst sort of cheater. I went home and talked to my da', seeking his advice on what to do and he told me something very important. It has stuck with me all these years, now I pass it to you, lad. 'Marriage is a long hard journey. It's not just frolics in the sun and making love on the beach. You have to fight for it. It's too easy to give up and if you're with the wrong one you *will* give up and then you will be miserable. But if you are with the right one, the one God has given you, it won't be any less difficult, but you might enjoy the journey a little more.' I knew Caitlin was the one I wanted and even though..." his dad broke off and cleared his throat.

"Even though I lost her, she gave me all of you. And I have been blessed with Deirdre. She's never tried to take Caitlin's place in my heart but, by god, that woman has burrowed her own path and place to where I cannot imagine being without her. So, I say to you, son, choose wisely and don't choose simply because you feel you have no choice. Trust me when I say, it's hard enough with the one you love, but it will be excruciating with the one you don't."

Sean didn't respond immediately. Finally, "do you think Trish is the right one for me?" Sean asked.

"*That* I cannot answer," Orin replied. "It is something you must decide, lad. But I think, if you're questioning it, it's something to ponder. Now, I love you, your family loves you. We will support you no matter what decision you make. If you decide you want Trish and you go through with the wedding next week, we will love her as one of our own. But, if you should decide you do not want this wedding, there is nothing done that cannot be undone. I do not want you to think of the money or the hurt for anyone but you. What is it that Sean Patrick O'Quinn wants? That is something only you can answer."

Orin gently stroked his son's face, smiled, and took a deep breath. "Now," he said dropping his hand. "Keera was out of line. She owes you an apology. Are you willing to come back to the Mill and finish your lunch?"

Nodding, he followed his father back into the restaurant. He would have plenty of time to think about what he wanted later. He would ask to trade places with Cabhan on the drive back. Being alone in the third seat of Emmet's car and away from Keera and especially Ness, was exactly what he needed.

"Hiya! Anyone home?" A female voice called out as the front door opened. Trish and Innis turned toward the closed door of his room. Panicked, they both jumped out of the bed and rushed about trying to find their clothes in order to be halfway presentable. "Hello? Trish? Innis?"

"Ah, hell, it's Rachael," Innis stated.

Cabhan's wife called out again, "Innis? Trish?"

"How does she know we're together?" Innis whispered harshly pulling on his jeans.

"More to the point what is she doing here?" Trish demanded. "Where's my bra?" She looked frantically around the room. Innis bent to pick it up off the floor and tossed it to her.

"Innis?" Rachael called again.

"Yeah, give me a sec, Rae," Innis called out. He threw on a t-shirt. "Wait here, I'll distract her. Try to get out of the window. Come around to the front like you just got home."

"You expect me to crawl out of the window?" Trish demanded.

"What are you doing in bed at this hour?" Rachael called down the hall.

"Just do it, woman," Innis hissed pulling her into him and kissing her roughly. Her fingers buried themselves into his hair as she melded to him. He tore away from her and headed to the door. Glancing back, "table linens, seamstress down in the village," he whispered. She nodded and pulled on her shoes.

Innis shut the door behind him and headed down the hallway to see his sister-in-law. Before he got there, his five-year-old niece ran to him squealing his name. Grinning, he picked her up and twirled her around, settling her on his hip.

"Well, hello stranger," Rachael smiled standing in the living room.

"You look good, Rae," he said kissing her cheek.

"I know, I know Cabhan is a lucky man," she winked and lovingly caressed her seven-month pregnant stomach. "And this one has been a little angel recently."

"Have you found out what it is?" Innis asked.

"A boy," she grinned.

"Grand," he smiled at her. "I know Cabh wanted another one."

"Oh trust me, I know. But I told him no more after this one. But I have a feeling he'll be able to convince me otherwise."

Innis chuckled. "Have you picked out a name?"

"We've settled on my great-grandda's name; Oisín."

"Oisín O'Quinn, sounds like a movie star," he winked.

"That's what I said," Rachael glowed. "So, I came over because on his way to Blarney, Cabhan called saying you and Trish were alone and might need some help planning a wedding. Since I've been through it, he thinks I can help. Men," she rolled her eyes but beamed. "This was the first moment I've been able to get here."

"No worries," Innis smiled tightly. "Trish actually had an appointment earlier with a seamstress for something or other. I was just taking a quick nap. The drive from Dublin was catching up with me."

"Oh, I'm sorry," she said. "Can I make you some coffee?"

"Nah, it's all right. I'm glad to see you," he set his niece down and motioned to the couch and chairs. "Did Cabhan say when they'd be back?"

"I heard they wanted to go to Killarney for drinks before coming home, so probably not until late," she said sitting in one of the chairs and handing her daughter some of her toys to play with. "How's everything going with the wedding?"

"Good, I think, yeah," he answered. "It would help if Sean was a little more active, but I think Trish is happy."

"At least you're here for her," she replied. "I bet you

handle all her needs." Innis shifted uncomfortably. "Now when will your turn be?"

"For what?"

"For marriage. What did you think I meant?"

"Oh, I don't know... women's minds are tricky waters to navigate."

"Women's minds?" she laughed. "You men think with the wrong brain and basically have one thing on your minds. Which reminds me... asleep in the middle of the day? Who is she, Innis? Did I scare her out of the window?"

"What?" Innis yelped.

"You're an adult. I'm not your mother. You don't have to hide your conquests from me."

"I have no idea what you're talking about, Rae," he said. "I wasn't," he glanced at his niece, then lowered his voice. "*With* anyone. I was simply asleep."

"She wore you out then?" she teased. Innis opened his mouth to say something but closed it almost immediately. "All right, you don't want to talk about it, I understand. But I'd like to see you with someone serious," she said.

"That's just not for me, Rae," he replied. "I'm not Cabhan or Sean."

"Hmm... it's a pity," she said. "You'd make a fine husband to a very lucky woman. And a wonderful father."

Before he could reply, the front door opened, and Trish walked in.

"Rachael!" she smiled. "It's good to see you." The little five-year-old girl ran to Trish and hugged her leg before going back to her toys.

"Was it a success?" Innis asked, not realizing he had

stood with nervous energy the second she walked in.

"Hardly," Trish replied. "Completely the wrong pattern. But she says she'll have it right in two days."

Innis nodded. Silence stretched and only after a moment did Innis realize they hadn't dropped each other's gaze.

"Can I get you a drink, Rae? Trish?" Innis forced.

"A glass of wine would be great," Trish replied.

"Gotcha," Innis said. "Rae?"

"Water for me please, at least for another two months," she smiled.

Innis went to the bar around the corner and out of Rae's line of sight. He could give the whole thing away if he wasn't careful. Taking a deep breath, he pulled down a glass and poured some red wine for Trish, the only wine she'd drink. He realized before he walked back out, even that small knowledge could be misread.

"We only have red, Trish. Is that all right?" he called out, covering as much as he could.

"Grand," she answered.

"Inn, you know that's all she drinks, ya crazy," Rae laughed.

Swallowing, he felt seventeen again like he had been caught by Ma with a girl or dirty magazines. His hands shook and his stomach was in knots. Pouring himself a glass of whiskey, he gulped it down. Then poured another and carried it out with the others.

Chapter

Eighteen

Orin, Deirdre, and Siobhan said goodbye in Blarney Town and took Cabhan's children home. The rest decided to head to Killarney for dinner and a pint or two. The grand little town of Killarney was so perfect in Ness's mind. Bustling with a big city feel but quiet and quaint as a small village with a cobblestoned main street. Emmet pulled into a parking spot near the Plaza hotel and since no one really wanted dinner, yet Emmet proposed a little sightseeing. There was a nature park in the heart of Killarney and with enough daylight left, they took the path that led into the preservation. Sean walked by himself behind Keera and Cabhan. Ness and Emmet led the way.

"What's the Ring of Kerry?" Ness asked as they passed a traffic sign.

"Ah, it has some of the most beautiful sights in the Kingdom," he said. "Kerry is known as the Kingdom, you know. It's almost a peninsula, like, and the outskirts of the county have some of the most picturesque landscapes and mountains you'll ever see."

"Oh, I get it, a ring around the peninsula," Ness offered.

"Exactly. There's the Skelligs, the old town of Sneem – used a lot on postcards, brightly painted houses and such – then there's Waterville, Lothar, Derrynane, Caherdaniel and Carroll's Cove, oh and we can't forget Ladies' View, some of the most beautiful views in all of Ireland. I'd be happy to take ya. It's a good day's drive to see it all. But if we start out early, we should be home before nightfall."

"I'd love to! What are the Skelligs?" she asked.

"Oh them? You'll love 'em, but I'll tell you about those later. Now, are ye ready for what's hidden around the bend?" he asked.

Ness looked at him confused but nodded and kept walking beside him.

The bend was a two-mile hike to the heart of the preservation. But when Ross Castle came into view, Sean's eyes were on Ness, not the scenery.

The castle loomed high in the pre-dusk sky. A ruined fortress sitting on a little inlet by the lake and rivers. The view was breathtaking. Mountain peaks graced the background of the scene lending their glory and majesty to the view around them. The fortress itself looked slightly burned or discolored. The light granite colored stones that made up the square keep, came to a point at the top of one of the corners. The outer bawn wall skirted the castle, showing its invulnerability while two round flanking towers faced the water. With the setting sun casting its' pink, red, yellow, and purple glow, the ancient castle was bathed in mystery, beauty, and absolute majesty.

Eventually Ness took her eyes off the building and landscape to read the information sign in front of her. Sean walked up, noticing her stiffen. He said nothing at first, only thrust his hands into the front pockets of his jeans and stared at the sign. It's English and Irish translation tempted him and soon he began reading part of the information in Irish.

Once he finished, she still wouldn't look at him. "That was lovely," she finally said. "How long have you been studying?"

"Since primary school," he explained. "I'm still learning. Irish is a living language so it's constantly changing."

"You have a good ear for it."

"Thank you. It's a beautiful language."

"Ness," Emmet called. "Come on over here! Come look inside!"

Cabhan and Keera went for a walk further into the woods around them. Emmet disappeared through the archway of the keep looking out across the inlet of Lough Léin. Sean trailed behind Ness at what he thought was a safe distance. It didn't help that her hair was billowing in the wind or that her shrug flapped about her as she walked, he knew he was done for. All the way to Killarney, he battled with himself. He just couldn't get her or his feelings out of his head.

He wanted her, and only her. As a sudden surge of strength coursed through him, he grasped her hand gently and gave it a gentle tug. Ness said nothing only went with him to the back of the castle. He gently pushed her against the wall and watched fire ignite in her eyes.

Chapter

Nineteen

Ness was in Heaven. That was the only explanation for it. She was standing amidst some of the most beautiful scenery she'd ever imagined with the stones of a ruined castle at her back and the man of her dreams setting her world on fire as the sun slowly set behind the mountains. For a moment she enjoyed it. Her heart pounded in her chest and under her hands she felt his heartrate accelerate. Still, he kissed her.

Then, pure dread filled her. She wasn't that sort of person. Sean was getting married. She hated herself for wanting him, but she would not allow him to cheat on his fiancée for her. Pushing him away, she whimpered when he pulled back. He stared at her, his eyes nearly black with pleasure.

"We can't, Sean," she said.

"I'm sorry," Sean breathed. "I shouldn't have done

that. I just can't get you out of my head," he lowered his forehead to hers.

"It's the same with me, Sean," she replied. "I have never felt like this with anyone but I won't let you ruin anything between you and Trish. She doesn't deserve it. She's loyal to you and I won't let you compromise your principles."

Sean's eyelids tightened around his closed eyes. "Ever since Trish and I first met we were just friends, best friends. But everyone kept saying how great we were. I thought it was all I should want. I was never blissfully happy with her. I care about her, of course, but I never have felt an all-encompassing want or need to be with her. I honestly don't know if I'm even attracted to her. I don't feel for her what I'm meant to be feeling."

"Don't say that," Ness replied. "In a week you'll be married, and I'll be heading back home."

"You can't," he breathed.

"I won't be here to make you question your resolve," she said. "There's nothing between us, Sean. There *can't* be."

Slowly, he opened his eyes. "You deserve to be loved," Sean said. "And by someone not afraid to love you."

She pressed her lips together and squeezed her eyes shut. "If I can give you nothing else," he started. "Let me give you this moment together."

Opening her eyes, she clutched his shirt. "No," she said resolutely. "We need to stop. Now. We should never have let it start. Let me go."

"Sean? Ness?" They heard Emmet call.

Sean pulled back, wiped his lips, and straightened his shirt. Ness did the same, just as Emmet walked around the corner.

Emmet stopped in his tracks. "Should I come back?"

"No," Ness smiled at him. "We were just talking."

"Oh, sure. Ehm... the sun's setting. I figured it would be best to head on out?"

"I'll call Cabhan and let him know," Sean said pulling out his phone.

"No need," Emmet replied. "I saw he and Keera start back a few minutes ago."

"Right, then let's go," Sean said.

Ness wrapped her arms around herself and without a glance at Sean, walked toward Emmet. They started the hike back to the main street shops for dinner.

Tyler lost them when they headed into Killarney's park. He waited near the town square across from the main gate. Seeing a man and a woman who had walked in with Ness leave and head down to a pub, he knew Ness couldn't be too far behind. He was right. About twenty minutes later, he saw her. Her lips were swollen like someone had taken care to kiss her senseless. It made his blood boil. She was his. If he couldn't have her, no one would. Eyeing Emmet, there was nothing to show he had kissed her. But then another man appeared behind them. The man Tyler had heard Ness call Sean. His lips were a bright rosy color and he watched Ness walking with Emmet.

Tyler clenched his fists at his side. His nails bit into the skin of his palm. He had attacked the wrong man. Sean was the one who was taking her away from him. Sean was the one who was showing her everything Tyler wanted to show. Sean was the one taking everything Tyler wanted to take. *Sean will die*, was his last thought before following them into a pub.

Sheehan's pub was exactly what Ness expected for an Irish pub. The long but narrow design had the bar to the left and seating to the right. Quaint, cozy, and completely Irish.

They found Cabhan and Keera already seated at a table on the two step raised platform, tucked in the back.

"We were lucky," Cabhan said as they walked up. "A group was leaving when Keera and I got here. Sorry it's a little tucked away."

"I'm not complaining," Emmet said sitting down on one of the padded stools. "Hoo... I forgot how long that walk was, my legs are like jelly."

"It was your idea," Sean laughed.

"I know, I know," he replied. "Take pity on your old brother, rub my feet, Sean."

"Lay off," Sean teased back pushing Emmet's boot off his knee.

"All right, folks, what can I get you?" Cabhan stood.

"This round is on me," Ness said pulling out her wallet. "The guys and I made a compromise."

"Yeah but you didn't make one with me," Cabhan grinned.

"Then you get your own," she laughed. "I've got everyone else's."

"Oh, I'm feelin' the love, cheers," he chuckled.

"I'm just saying," she teased.

"All right," Cabhan laughed. "A compromise with me then. I buy the first round, you get the second."

"Are all of you O'Quinn men into compromises?" she sighed.

"Yeah pretty much," Cabhan answered simply.

"Fine," she gave up and put her purse away. "Then I'll have a beer."

"What kind?" he asked.

"Surprise me," she offered.

"Probably a pilsner," Emmet said to Cabhan.

"Harp?" Cabhan questioned.

"I actually prefer a Killians or Smithwicks," Ness replied. "So, a red would be best or a Belgian."

Emmet looked over, impressed. "Well, look at you."

Once Cabhan left, Keera looked over at Sean. "Sean, I'm really sorry. I shouldn't have said what I did."

Nodding once, he answered. "Thank you, Kee. It's all right. It's over and done. Thank you for your apology."

"I just love you and want you happy. Tell me you're happy and I'll not say another word."

Sean couldn't keep eye contact with his cousin when he answered, "yeah, I'm happy."

They were quiet for a time then Keera leaned forward, speaking to Ness. "So, I know it's kinda been nonstop for you so far, Ness. But when would you want to go to Dublin with us?"

"Oh, um..." she started. "I know Emmet said there's some wedding stuff there this week."

Emmet smiled. "We'll be heading over on Wednesday. You and Trish will already be there, Sean?"

"No, we'll all be leaving at the same time," Sean said.

"Where's the rehearsal dinner again?" Keera asked.

"A Guinness Canal Barge," he said.

"Grand! That'll be so fun! Love the city at night! So romantic! You'll love it, Ness," Keera replied.

"Oh well, Kee, I wasn't invited," Ness said.

"Sean, she's my plus one," Keera replied.

"I don't think Trish would appreciate that," Ness's voice trailed off.

"What are you gonna be doing while we're there? You'll be bored. Come on." Keera asked. "Ah, there's Cabhan."

Ness looked up to see him balancing three pints of Guinness in one hand, another in the other along with Killians, and some napkins. Emmet helped him out by taking one from either hand and setting them down.

"Cheers, Cabhan," Keera said grabbing hers.

"No worries," he grinned sitting down and raising his Guinness. "Sláinte!"

"Sláinte," they replied clinking glasses.

"What's that mean?" Ness asked after they drank.

"Cheers," Sean explained. "Or *to your health*."

"Now, they said the music is about to start. If we want anything to eat, we'd better order it now," Cabhan said after taking another hefty swallow from his Guinness.

"Oh, well, I'm fine," Ness replied.

"You've not eaten much all day," Sean leaned forward.

"I had a great lunch. But I wouldn't say not to some appetizers," Ness said.

"Come on up to the bar with me, there's no table service in Ireland," Sean and Ness stood from the table and toward the bar.

Once Sean and Ness were out of ear shot, the three remaining at the table, leaned in.

"It's not working," Cabhan said. "Sean's too pigheaded."

"No, he's being loyal," Emmet answered.

"To a woman who is cheating on him with our brother. How can he not see it?" Cabhan demanded.

"I know," Keera hissed. "And Ness is too shy to come out and say she likes him."

"I saw them kissing on the side of Ross Castle, but I don't think he'll do it again," Emmet said. "I heard Ness say they need to stop."

Cabhan huffed but took another drink. "One thing is for certain, Rachael called me just a bit ago, Kee was with me," he explained. "She went to the house after I gave her a call and Innis was still in bed. Trish came in through the front door a short time later but they were both flushed, lips red as a rose, stumbling over their cover, and looking guilty as hell. They are *absolutely* sleeping together."

"Dammit, how could Innis do that to our brother?" Emmet demanded.

"I don't think he's thinking of Sean when he's bonking Trish," Keera replied. Sighing harshly, she looked at both of her cousins "We can't just tell him. You saw what happened when I tried."

"I was surprised you were so forthright with it,"

Cabhan said.

"Someone had to be," she answered. "After what I saw them doing? They didn't realize I was watching them through the window when they sucked face."

Cabhan nearly choked on his beer. "Jaysus, Kee."

"What? It's what they did! I thought I was going to be sick. Innis is my favorite of all of you."

"Oh right, tanks very much," Emmet stated.

"Well, there's now a vacancy for that position," she replied.

"Cheers, so what now?" Emmet asked.

"Maybe they could get together in Dublin, take Ole Bess and she could *accidentally* have a malfunction and they have to walk. Dublin's a romantic city," Keera said. "You work on cars, Emmet couldn't you take care of it?"

"I sell cars, there's a difference," Emmet replied.

"Then Uncle Orin," she said. "We all know that boat will never run again. He's gotta know a few things about sabotage."

Emmet said. "It'll never work, Kee."

"Let's think about it," Cabhan replied. "They're coming back from the bar now." Leaning back, Cabhan continued speaking as if they were talking about the latest hurling match. "I think that our lads have the best chance."

"What's that now?" Sean asked.

"Of beating Clare," Emmet provided.

"Now you just wait a minute there, mister," Keera said. "*My* lads have never let me down."

"Sorry, what are you guys talking about?" Ness asked.

"The hurling game where Kerry will grind Clare to a pulp," Emmet raised his glass in cheers as some of the other patrons overheard and shouted their agreement.

"I'm sorry, lads," Keera said in a singsongy voice. "Just you wait until Friday, you'll be crying at the pub when they lose."

"You know those are fighting words, Miss," a handsome stranger smiled at her.

Keera eyed him. "I wouldn't mind fighting with you."

The stranger smirked. "Buy you a drink?" he asked.

Keera pushed her Guinness towards Sean. "Why not?" Sliding out of the booth, she took his hand.

Emmet, Cabhan and Sean all shook their heads, even though they were smiling.

"Patrick O'Flannery," Cabhan sighed. "Gotta watch those lads."

"You know him?" Ness asked.

"Cabhan knows everyone," Emmet chuckled.

"So, um, what's hurling?" she asked.

"It's the national sport," Emmet explained. "There's deathly rivalries between the counties. It's kinda like field hockey, American football, and lacrosse all rolled into one."

"Sounds dangerous," she said.

"Ehm," he debated, taking a drink of his Guinness. "Can be. I used to play at University." He pulled back his floppy hair to show a scar on his forehead just where his hairline ended. "Got this from one of the sticks."

"Did it hurt?" Ness gasped.

"Bleed a whole hell of a lot, but no damage," he said.

"Ya don't stop, ya just keep on playing. Didn't know I was hurt until the blood started dripping in my eyes obstructing my sight."

She grimaced. Emmet chuckled and leaned back in his seat. One of the women who worked at the pub, came towards their table.

"Compliments from the man at the bar," she replied setting down a plate and walking away.

Ness went pale when she stared at the food.

"Ness?" Emmet called, but she didn't reply nor lift her eyes from the food.

The fries were covered in blue cheese, onions, and bacon. Her cheeks turned red and her breathing quickened.

"I have to get out of here," she said.

"Ness?" Emmet and Sean questioned. She didn't look at them only rushed through the crowd. But there were too many people, she couldn't get out. Pushing everyone out of the way, Emmet and Sean watched as she ran out of the pub.

"Go," Emmet ordered his brother.

Sean didn't hesitate and raced after her.

Chapter

Twenty

"Ness!" someone yelled. She stumbled on the cobblestones and nearly fell to her knees. But someone was there. He wrapped his arms around her and held her close to him, preventing her from falling. She clutched at his arms around her waist, hitting and kicking at him, demanding he let her go.

"Nessa, it's me," he said at her ear.

"Let me go!" she screamed.

"It's Sean," he said again. "You're safe."

Even though his words registered in her mind, all she could feel were her stepfather's arms around her shoulders, his disgusting mouth on hers and the way his tongue snaked out when he tried to kiss her. She could taste the loaded French fries he had had at the bar, the cheese sauce still caked on the side of his mouth. She was going to throw up.

Breaking away from Sean, she quickly rushed to a patch of grass beside the church across the street. Sean was right on her heels and clutched her shoulders as dry heaves wracked her body.

Sean's soothing voice helped her calm down. She held on to the reality he represented. Eventually, the heaves ended and she turned into him. Her eyes were watering, either from tears or the pain of gagging, she wasn't sure. Sean wiped the wetness on her face away as he kissed her hair lightly.

"Sit down," he said leading her to a bench.

"I'm sorry," she finally said as she tried to breathe deeply, clearing her mind of the imagined smell and taste.

"Shh," he replied gently.

"I don't know what came over me," she went on.

"I swear I will kill that man if I get my hands on him," he said softly.

"No!" she reared back to look at him shocked. "No! This is not your fight."

"I'm making it mine."

"And when you're married? When Trish is pregnant? Will you fight my battles still?"

"Listen to me, Nessa," he cupped her face. "I will never let him hurt you again."

"Sean," she breathed and shook her head.

"The wedding is off. I will not marry her," he replied. "I'm falling for you, Ness. I refuse to lie to myself or her."

"You don't even know me," she breathed.

"I want to," he said. "I want to get to know you. I'm not saying marry me next month. But I can't marry someone else when all I want is you. This feeling. I have never understood my da's metaphor of lightning when he met my mother and ma, but now I do. I know what it means with you, Ness."

"Sean," she sighed. "I can't. There are too many things in my past. I just need to keep running. I won't mess up your future."

"No," Sean said. "You can't run forever."

He pressed his mouth to hers, demanding, branding, seducing. Wanting a chance to get away from her world, needing to know what happiness felt like, even for a moment, Ness gave in and raised her hand. Digging her nails into the short cropped brown hair on the back of his head, making him groan, she grew far too fond of his kisses. Something in the pit of her stomach churned with nervous energy.

She tried to force herself to pull back, but she couldn't. It was like they were made for each other. Her heart swelled as she thought about the man kissing her. He was everything she ever dreamed of. Loving, kind, protective and sexy. He appealed to her in a way no other man had, and she never wanted to imagine what it would feel like to give him up or to never again share his kiss.

Sean couldn't believe how he felt about Ness. She was everything he never knew he wanted. As he sat on the bench, kissing her, he was the one going senseless. She melded perfectly to him and finally he understood his father's warning. He did not want to stop short of making her his in every way possible.

"Sean?" A woman's voice behind him made his stomach jump. He froze, then tore his mouth away from Ness and turned.

His future in laws stood on the cobblestones, staring at him. Sean let out a soft curse.

"What the bloody hell is going on here, lad?" his future father-in-law demanded.

Sean closed his eyes for a moment as his heart rate sped up as dread filled him.

"Brenda, Dermott," Sean said looking over at them. "This... ehm... isn't what you think."

"And just what do we think, lad?" Trish's father demanded, his face turning red.

"Ehm..." Sean wracked his brain and turned to look at his mother-in-law's hazel eyes. "This is Ness. She's a friend of my cousin Keera. She's... coming to the wedding."

"Is she?" Brenda, Trish's mother, said sharply, crossing her arms over her chest defensively. "I don't think so. I'm not sure there should even be a wedding now."

"Please," Sean said softly. "She was scared I was just..."

"Cheating on our daughter," Dermott supplied.

Sean took a deep breath, swallowed hard and stood. "It got out of hand," Sean apologized. "It won't happen again."

"How long has this been going on?" Brenda demanded.

"Nothing is going on," Sean replied.

"Didn't look like it to us," Dermott said.

"Ehm..." Sean was at a loss.

"It was my fault," Ness stood and walked in front of Sean. "I... um..."

"This is on both of you," Dermott interrupted harshly.

Under the Irish Sky

"Sean, how dare you do this to our daughter!"

"It's not like that," Sean replied.

"Then how is it? Were we hallucinating? Were you *not* kissing this girl?" Dermott demanded.

Sean shrugged and figured the truth was always best.

"Yeah," he answered. "I was."

"Sean," Ness breathed.

"We can't deny it," he replied. Turning back, Brenda was pale and staring at Ness. "Yes, I was kissing her, but it was a mistake." He hated himself for saying it but he needed to talk to Trish first. "I will be speaking to Trish as soon as I get home and explain the situation. The wedding, as far as I am concerned, is still on." He couldn't look at Ness, but he knew she was running.

ChapCER

CwENCy-ONE

He lied to her. He didn't care for her at all. She was a distraction from his pre-wedding jitters. She meant nothing to him and here she had given him her first kiss. She should have known. Giving a little bit of herself, and all he did was rip her heart out, throw it on the ground and stomp on it as she watched helplessly from the sidelines.

Never again! Ness swore.

It was over. Deciding to seal up her heart and never let another living soul inside. *Okay, that's dramatic.* She thought. Her heart felt like it would burst out of her chest. The pain was intense. Crying wasn't an option. She'd never give him the satisfaction. If she did cry, it would be by herself where no one could use it against her.

"Ness!" She heard. His voice made her angry.

Oh no, Mr. O'Quinn you're not getting me again.

"Ness, wait up, will ya!" Sean called. She felt his fingers grab her wrist. Twirling around, her left hand had a mind of its own. He stumbled back when her hand connected with his cheek. "Bloody hell! What was that for?"

"What do you think?"

"What did you expect me to do? Those were Trish's parents!"

"I know!" She shouted. "But God! You should never have kissed me!"

"That's what this is about?" He was confused.

"You told me you were falling for me. You made me fall in love with you. And now this?"

Sean was quiet a moment. "You love me?" he finally said.

"Oh, don't be such a moron!"

"Look, I didn't want them calling Trish. I wanted to tell her myself."

"It doesn't matter anymore! It's over! You made your choice!"

"What are you talking about?" He demanded. "I haven't made any choice."

"You did when you told them the wedding is still on," Ness said.

"I said that for their benefit!"

"It doesn't matter! You two deserve each other." She wanted to hurt him, not intentionally, but so he felt the same pain she felt. It wasn't fair. "I want a man, not a boy too afraid to stand up to a woman. Go! Be miserable! Go marry that cheater! You know, I didn't want to say anything, but I saw your brother Innis and your precious fiancée kissing! That's right, a real lip locker, his tongue was pretty much halfway down her throat. It was disgusting! I wasn't going to say anything but now I'm tired of being the sweet, innocent, little girl that people feel sorry for but walk all over! No more! I'm done! I've been crushed too many times by men, and this is it! It's over!"

She ran back to the pub leaving him speechless.

Entering Sheehan's, Ness found Emmet standing near the music group singing along with a beer in his hand. He met her gaze and winked. But then, seeing the look in her eyes, he stopped singing and mouthed *what happened?*

Motioning him over, he made his way through the crowd. She started to say something, but he shook his head and motioned to the door. Setting his beer on the entryway table, he followed her out. They walked down the street towards the Plaza Hotel.

"What happened?" he asked, placing comforting hands on her arms.

"He... we... Trish's parents... oh god, Emmet!" She lost control of what little composure she had left and fell into his arms. Burying her face into his chest she muffled her scream. Wrapping his arms around her, he held her tightly.

After a little while, he stroked her arms, "hey, Ness," he breathed quietly. "Come on, girl. Tell me what happened."

She tried to gain control of her emotions and eventually was able to pull away. He smiled down at her.

"Oh, Emmet," she wailed and buried her head into his chest again. "Why can't more guys be like you?"

"Eh, where's the fun in that? I'm one of a kind," he chuckled.

She laughed and looked up at him. "God, you always know what to say to make me laugh," she said wiping her tears.

"Now, love," he started. "What happened?"

She proceeded to tell him everything that happened after Sean chased her out of the pub. She could tell he tried very hard not to react, but she felt him tense.

"Could you take me home, Emmet?" She finally asked. "Or tell me where to get a taxi?"

"I'll take you home, girl," he gently stroked his knuckles across on her cheek. "But are you sure you want to go right now? Trish will be there and from what you've told me, I think it would be best to get some distance between you and Sean."

"Oh god," she sighed. "I have nowhere to go. I should never have come here! I should just go home!"

He chuckled, "and you say you're not Irish. One extreme to the other in a matter of two seconds."

"I'm glad I amuse you," she replied sarcastically.

"Oh, come now," he said. "Listen, we'll just hang out for a couple of days, then go to Dublin. Can you handle hanging out with me for that time?"

She nodded. "I feel safe around you, Emmet."

"Phew!" He exaggerated. "Yes! And it only took," he looked at his watch. "Four days." He looked back and winked.

"Shut up," she grinned and punched his shoulder.

"Ow," he pretended. Laughing, he pulled her to him, kissed her hair and rubbed his hand up and down her arms quickly warming her. "Come on, girl, let me give Cabhan the keys to my car. That's Killarney Plaza Hotel. One of the best hotels in Kerry. We'll get two rooms and book a couples massage," he winked.

"Sounds amazing," she laughed. "But how expensive is it? I have money but probably not that much."

Emmet stood and held out his hand to her. "Go on in and tell 'em Emmet O'Quinn sent you and we need two rooms for tonight and tomorrow. Make sure they're near each other," he said. "I'll just pop back into Sheehan's and give Cabhan the keys."

Emmet watched her go into the hotel and turned back to Sheehan's. Luckily, he had told her to pack a change of clothes, but he knew that wasn't going to be enough for a couple of days. They would have to go shopping. Making a mental note to ask Keera to pack Ness a bag for the Dublin trip, he walked back into the pub. Pulling Cabhan out the back door to the back stairs, the door between them cutting down on the music, Emmet told Cabhan what happened.

Cabhan sighed harshly. "That stupid boy. What was he thinking?"

"Sometimes I wonder whose child he really is," Emmet said. "He's too…"

"Stubborn?" Cabhan supplied.

"Yeah."

"And you wonder whose brother he is?" Cabhan looked pointedly at him.

"Shut it," he said.

"I'm glad the girl's taken an interest in you," Cabhan went on. "Are you sure you'll be all right with that madman out there?"

"Yeah, no worries," Emmet said. "I'll call you when I'm in my room. We can talk more then."

"Good," Cabhan answered.

They both turned when they heard someone coming up the stairs from the basement restrooms. Sean appeared and his brothers noticed the fading hand shaped red mark on his face.

"What are you doing?" Emmet asked.

"What the hell does it matter to you?" Sean demanded.

"Stop acting like an arse," Emmet replied.

"Don't talk to me about being an arse, Emmet," Sean answered coming closer to him, itching for a fight. Cabhan stepped between his two brothers.

"Sean, enough," he said. "Go back inside. Emmet, stop baiting him."

"Don't tell me what to do. I'm not a child," Sean answered.

"Just go," Cabhan ordered.

Having grown up with Cabhan fourteen years older, they knew Sean hated how Cabhan could be like a father. It was something he rarely used, but the situation called for it. Glaring at him, Sean went back into the pub.

"Here are my keys," Emmet replied. "Tell Keera to call me so I can tell her what needs to be done. Could you go to my place and pack me a bag? And take Jacks to ma and da's?" His black Labrador wasn't needed but he wasn't expecting to stay overnight, and Jacks would need to be let out and fed.

"Yeah, I gotcha," Cabhan answered.

"Cheers," Emmet said. "I'd better get back to Ness. She's probably got our rooms. Call me later?"

"Will do as soon as I get home," Cabhan replied. "I guess the whole plan back fired, huh?"

"That's an understatement," Emmet answered. "But it would have worked had Sean not been so stubborn or blind to the truth."

Cabhan nodded and waved as Emmet left through the side door. Everything that was supposed to happen, protecting his brother, helping Ness, fixing what Innis and Trish had destroyed, nothing worked. It was over.

Chapter

Twenty-Two

Emmet found Keera outside the pub smoking with the O'Flannery lads. His look of displeasure was enough to make her flinch and throw the cigarette down. Snuffing it out with her foot, she headed over to her cousin.

"When did that start up again?" Emmet demanded.

"Don't start, Em," she replied. "You're no' me da'."

"No, I'm not," he answered. "I'm your cousin and I'm worried about you." Keera waved her hand in a gesture of dismissal. "Kee, I'm serious. I thought you quit," he continued.

"It was a stressful last semester, lay off," she replied.

"Does your ma know?" Emmet asked.

Keera paled and took a step closer to him. "Ya can't tell her, Emmet, swear. She'd tan my hide for sure," she begged.

"Promise me you'll quit and prove to me you're serious then just maybe, I won't tell her. I will give you five days."

"You've gotta give me more time," she pleaded.

"Five days, Keera," he said sternly.

"Fine, ye bloody plonker," she huffed.

"Hey," he raised his voice in discipline. "Do not speak to me like that. I may be your cousin, but I am older than you and I used to mind you as a child. You will respect me as your elder. Jaysus, Keera," he sighed running his hand through his hair. "Look," he sighed. "You know I love ya, girl. I just don't want to see ya hurting yourself like that, all right?"

"A single cigarette with friends is not going to kill me, Em," she said.

He sighed. She didn't understand. He knew the dangers of addiction and what just *one little cigarette with friends* could lead to. If he could prevent anyone, especially a loved one from going through what he went through, he would.

"Just forget it, Keera," he sighed. "You're like a sister to me. I just don't want anything to happen to you. I'll give you until the wedding to stop."

"Fine, Emmet," she snapped. "Now, what the hell did you want me for?"

Walking down the street to a bench, Emmet explained what had just occurred and saw Keera visibly flinch.

"Sean, that bloody eejit," she breathed. "What do we do now?"

"Now," he sighed. "It's over, Kee. Nothing more can be done."

161

Keera sighed harshly. "Where's Ness?"

"At the Plaza," he replied hooking his thumb over his shoulder indicating the hotel. Keera bit her lip and nodded.

"I want to see her," she said and Emmet could see she was almost giddy.

Immediately going to her best friend, Keera threw her arms around her. Emmet walked up behind them and headed to the counter to speak to his friend Paddy.

"Men are gobshites, honey, I'm so sorry," Keera replied.

"Ach, tanks very much," Emmet replied while Paddy behind the counter muttered a sarcastic *cheers.*

"Emmet told me what happened," Keera went on. "I can't believe that arsehole!"

"Kee, it's okay," Ness soothed.

"No, it's not," Keera said. "But listen, I'll pack you some things when I get back. We'll go down to Dublin and get us a couple hot barmen. We'll flirt the night away. Oh, and we'll have Emmet to make sure no guy gets too close."

"Oh?" Emmet asked. "And what if I want to leave early to have me own fun?"

Keera waved him off. "We all know you've been celibate since Chloe."

Emmet stared at her then began to chuckle. Paddy laughed outright. "Right," Emmet replied with a side glance at his friend. "'Cause *that's* normal."

"Anyway," Keera replied rolling her eyes. "Stay here for a little. Go see the Ring of Kerry and Emmet will look after you. Get Sean out of your head."

Ness nodded and tried to smile. Giving another tight hug, Keera gave Emmet a look and headed out. Almost immediately, Ness stepped into Emmet's arms.

"Did you want to go up to the rooms?" he asked after a moment. She nodded into his chest.

She looked up at him as they walked toward the elevator. "Why don't I want to be with you, Emmet? It would save me a lot of heartache."

"No' sure about that, love," Emmet chuckled. "I have me own set of problems. Come on. It's late and you've had a rough go of it."

All she could do was nod. He pushed the button to call the elevator car and wrapped his arm around her shoulders, hating the feeling of submission and surrender he felt in her body. She was running in fear of her life from a man who was supposedly dead and now her heart was breaking because of that stupidly, stubborn brother of his. She deserved to be loved, treated as a queen, and never heart hurt. But no, Sean was selfish and idiotic enough not to see what was staring him in the face. As his mind scolded his brother, a face flashed before his eyes and he sighed harshly.

You're one to talk, Emmet O'Quinn, he thought. *You did exactly the same thing to Chloe.* Closing his eyes, he blocked out the image of Chloe's tear stained face from ten years ago.

The interminable elevator ride finally came to an end with the soft ding and slight lurch of the car. Stepping out into the fourth-floor foyer, Emmet took a look at the numbers on the keycards and steered her towards the right, through the swinging double glass doors.

Finally, they stopped outside a corner room. Emmet unlocked the door and pushed it open. Ness walked in. Her arms were wrapped protectively around her.

Emmet stayed by the door. "The water bottles on the table are complimentary. The piano bar is down on the second floor. Didn't know if you wanted a drink." She shook her head. "Didn't think so. I'm gonna leave you the extra key to my room," he set it down on the desk. "And ya have my number if you need me."

"I think," her voice was soft. "I'll just take a bath and watch a little TV."

"It breaks me heart to see you like this, Ness," he said. "But trust me, I know it doesn't seem like it now, but it'll be all right."

"Promise?"

"With my record? No," he replied truthfully.

"At least *you* are honest with me," she answered.

He stared at her for a long time, then averted his eyes. "I'll leave you to your bath," he said and with that, left the room.

Chapter

Twenty-Three

Emmet lay on the queen size bed in his hotel room, reading an article on his phone. Making a mental note to call his broker in the morning, he yawned as the words were getting blurry and his eyes were closing by themselves.

Suddenly, he was wide awake as the door to his room opened and Ness came into view.

"Ness, love, are you all right?" he asked. She nodded but looked down as if she was embarrassed. "What is it?" he asked gently.

"I… I couldn't sleep," she said. "I wondered… I'm sorry, it was stupid."

"It's not stupid," he replied, reaching over to the chair by his bed and pulling on his white t-shirt. He sat up and reached for her. "Would you want to stay here for a bit?" He offered.

"Would you mind?" she asked.

"No, not at all," he said pulling the sheets down for her. She hesitated for a moment. "I promise to behave like a gentleman."

"Right," came her embarrassed breathy reply.

"Ahh, come on, girl. I'm not accustomed to taking what is not mine. You are safe from my attentions... tonight," his eyes twinkled. She half smiled but slid into the sheets. Emmet held her close. "Now tomorrow might be different..."

She giggled and slightly slapped his chest.

"Oh ouch," he winked. "Now, seriously, go to sleep," he sounded anything but serious.

"I have never done this before," she whispered.

"Sleep? Well, no wondered you're Wonder Woman," he grinned.

"Shut up," she giggled.

"No' a chance," he grinned. "It's pretty simple," he said. "You pretty much have the hang of it."

"I kinda like you, Emmet," she laughed.

"Kinda?" he looked comically horrified.

"Okay... a lot, then," she replied.

"That's better," he smiled relaxing back on his pillow. "Everything will be all right, Ness, I promise. You are an amazing young woman. You deserve to be loved unconditionally. Sean is a fool. Trust me. I had one like you, and like an eejit, I let her go, thinking it was for her own good. I could never have been more wrong. I was scared and selfish. It's not easy for any man to admit it, but it's true.

"I know what it feels like. I know how your heart is

hurting, trust me. I hide behind this joker façade but that's just because I'm scared to let anyone else in. The last time I did, I wound up screwing it up and I never want to be the cause of a beautiful woman's tears again. I don't think I could handle it."

Ness let Emmet's words sink in as she felt him relax beside her; his breathing became slow and even as he fell asleep.

Snuggled in Emmet's arms, she finally felt safe. Moving to get a better look at him, she took in his features. He was so handsome.

His auburn hair was dark, almost brown and shaggy with a wave in its depths. She instinctively reached out to run her fingers through it. His high cheekbones chiseled his face like a romantic hero of old. He looked surprisingly younger and at peace when asleep. She moved her hand from his hair down to his long straight nose and halted when she felt a ridge where it had been broken. Her finger trailed down and fell on the bow of his upper lip. He moaned softly but didn't wake.

When he didn't move, she went back to studying his face. His lips were full but not in an unattractive way. It suited him and she had the strangest urge. Removing her finger, she leaned forward and brushed her lips against his. It felt strange, foreign, not in an unpleasant way but more of an unfamiliar way. Not at all how it felt with Sean. When she pulled back and opened her eyes, she was startled to see Emmet's eyes open, staring at her.

"Ness," he started softly. "What are you doing?"

His voice was cautious, not accusatory, but she felt like she had just been caught doing something awkward for them both.

"I... I," she started. "I'm sorry, Emmet. I was curious. I didn't mean to."

"Nessa," his voice was soft. "If you wanted to kiss me just ask. I'm sorry, love. I'm not interested in you like that but I'm hardly a prude."

Her cheeks flamed red. "I didn't mean to," she said. "I'm sorry."

"Don't be sorry, love," he replied. "You're confused and upset. I won't hold it against you."

"Tell me something, Emmet."

"Anything," he answered turning to get comfortable, resting on his back.

"Do you think Sean cared about me at all?"

"Aye, Ness, he cared about you," Emmet said. "He's just an eejit."

"Emmet," she started.

"Yeah?"

"I think I'm in love with him."

Chapter

Twenty-Four

Ness's body ached when she woke the next morning. Opening her eyes to the morning sun shining through the drapes, she stretched and looked beside her. She was alone. Sitting up quickly, her head pounding, she called for Emmet.

There was no answer. "Emmet?" she called again a little louder.

The bathroom door opened, and Emmet appeared, a white hotel towel wrapped around his hips. His hair was wet, and his face contorted into a concerned frown.

"Ness, love, you all right? What's wrong?" he asked.

"Uh?" she replied staring at his chiseled chest. She thought only movie stars had that kind of physique. A little smattering of dark red chest hair covered his upper torso, and looked as soft as the hair on his head. Six tight abs and two more disappearing below the towel, and the V at his hips she had heard Keera groan about on any action star, made up Emmet's chest and abdomen.

"Ness," he called. She finally looked up and saw the smirk toying with the right side of his lips. "My eyes are up here, love."

"Sorry," she blushed and looked down. "You're just… very nice to look at."

"You're not too bad yourself," he winked lifting another towel to his head, drying his ears. "You all right?"

"I didn't know where you were," she replied looking away. "I was worried."

"Shower, love," he answered motioning to the bathroom. She nodded and risked a glance back.

The muscles of his shoulders moved as he towel dried his hair, everything about him screamed power and for a moment, she fancied herself attracted to him. But once he raised his eyes to hers again, she dismissed the idea.

"But since you're awake… good morning. Did you sleep well?" He asked. She nodded. "Good, now why don't you get back to your room and get dressed? We'll catch some breakfast and then go raid the clothing store across the street. We can get an early start on the Ring. I want us to have lunch at the Skelligs. It's supposed to be a beautiful day today and we can come back here for dinner or try another pub around town."

"How expensive is this store we're going to?" she asked mentally calculating the money in her wallet.

"Average tourist trap," he shrugged wiping his chest. "But the clothes are good and the location is even better. We'll need to get a car too, I gave Cabhan my keys and I didn't bring my motorcycle."

"I'm sorry to be such a bother," she said.

"Hey," he sat down on the bed. "You're far from a bother, Ness." She smiled thanking him. "Now, let me finish drying off and getting dressed. I'll meet you by the elevators," he offered.

"Sounds good," she answered.

"Fifteen minutes?"

"Twenty? I need to shower too."

"Done."

Ness hurried down the hall to her corner room and ran the water in the shower. Happy she packed an extra pair of clothes, she pulled them out of her backpack and set them on her bed. Then jumping into the shower, she washed away the grim of the day before.

Twenty-five minutes later, Emmet saw Ness heading towards him.

"Ready?" he asked.

"I didn't realize the time, I'm sorry," Ness said.

"No worries."

"I still look a mess. My eyes match my hair," she laughed humorlessly, motioning to her bloodshot, tear reddened eyes.

"You look fine," he smiled warmly hitting the elevator button

"Em, I want you to know I know it's strange to feel the way I do for Sean without knowing him more than a few days but..."

"Trust me, I understand," Emmet replied. The

elevator dinged and the doors opened. "Breakfast first?" He asked. Almost on cue, her stomach growled. They both chuckled. "I'll take that as a yes," Emmet grinned and pressed the button for the second level.

"I haven't had anything since Blarney," she replied.

"God, girl that seems like a lifetime ago," he said.

"Trust me," she laughed humorlessly. "I know."

Stepping out of the elevator, she followed Emmet's lead to the breakfast room.

"Em," the same man she met the night before greeted them. "Breakfast for two?" he winked.

"Hey, Paddy, you've got it right but only on the first assumption. This is Ness, a family friend," Emmet said.

"Right, we met last night," Paddy smiled a knowing smile. "Pleasure, Ness."

"Hi," she replied.

"Well, you're in luck, breakfast is in full swing. Come on in," he took them toward a table near the windows. "I hope this joker has taken *good* care of you."

"Paddy," Emmet's voice was a warning. Paddy waved him off.

"He's been a great friend," Ness said.

"God, I love American accents," Paddy sighed, his eyes sparkled as he grinned at Emmet. Frowning fiercely at his friend, Emmet elbowed Paddy out of the way so he could help Ness into her seat.

"Thanks," she smiled up at him.

"If you need anything," Paddy was saying. "Anything at all, don't hesitate—"

"I know where everything is, Paddy," Emmet cut him off.

"Right, of course," he grinned. Eventually, Paddy left them alone.

"Ach, sorry about that, love," Emmet said.

"I always thought the Irish were shy about sex," she laughed.

"Paddy and I have known each other for a very long time. I used to work here," Emmet explained.

"Paddy," she said the name. Then her eyes grew wide. "Paddy O'Shea?"

Emmet's brows furrowed. "Aye. How do you know his name?"

She looked away, her cheeks heating. "I don't. Uhm, no reason. So you guys have been friends for a while? And you what? Would bring your conquests back here?" she asked bluntly. "He thinks I'm just another one of your women."

"Only because he has the past to go on, nothing more," Emmet replied.

"It's okay," she smiled. "Kinda made me feel good about myself, if he thinks a guy like you would be interested in me. That's kinda nice."

"A guy like me?" Emmet asked. "And what kinda of guy would that be?"

"You know," she looked down.

"Nah, I really don't."

"You're very handsome… funny, sweet, and gracious," she finally said.

"Shh," he winked. "Don't let that get out. I'd have to

swim through the women who would be after me." She giggled. "I'm very happy in my bachelorhood," he replied.

"Whoever gets you, Emmet," she began. "Will be the most fortunate girl in the world."

He smiled sweetly and reached across the table to take her hand. Bringing her fingers to his lips, they stared at each other for a moment.

"Come on," he said finally. "Let's get some food."

Chapter

Twenty-Five

"Oh my god," Ness breathed. "This is absolutely breathtaking."

Emmet grinned as he watched her gaze out over the water toward the Skelligs.

"I thought you might like it," he replied. She stood beside the dirt road staring across the Atlantic. The island mounds looked lonely and austere, with the sky slowly turning grey, as clouds rolled in from the west. Ness stood before him, her scarf, which Emmet had picked out earlier that day, whipped around her as the pre-storm winds stirred around them.

"Tell me about them," Ness begged.

"The islands are called the Skelligs," Emmet started. "Specifically, Skellig Michael," he pointed to the largest one. "This was considered the edge of the world by the earliest monks. They found the islands and decided that the seclusion, conditions, and the beauty of God's Island lent to their connection with Him. They chose this location to commune with God."

"It's a monastery?" she asked squinting to see the mounds miles off in the distance.

"Yes," he answered. "The earliest known, with over six hundred steps to the top."

"Can we go?" her eyes sparkled.

"If you'd like but I'll have to double check if they're running the ferry," he said. "And if that storm will be a deterrent. Let's go to the Centre? Have some lunch? They have an amazing Irish stew and there's a video we can watch all about the history, then to the gift shop. There's plenty more to see on the Ring but take your time."

"Sounds good to me," she replied. "I am hungry. What time is it?"

"About one," he answered offering his arm to her. His phone buzzed again in his back pocket. He wasn't sure if he could check it without Ness seeing.

Cabhan and Keera were keeping him up to date with a play by play of the conversation Sean was having with Trish. According to them, Trish had forgiven Sean his little indiscretion and the wedding was still on. But had yet to tell Sean about her affair with Innis.

After Emmet stopped at the front desk asking about the ferry, he looked for Ness. He found her resting her hands on the wooden banister, gazing out across the sea. He watched her for a moment.

"It is so beautiful," Ness said without turning.

"'Tis," Emmet answered.

"Sean's going through with the wedding, isn't he?"

"What makes you think that?"

"You looked at your phone earlier and I saw it in your eyes," she admitted.

"Ness, it has nothing to do with his feelings for you."

"I know," she answered. "I'm glad he's doing it. He hardly knows me and he's been with Trisha for a while. I was a distraction, nothing more."

"You're wrong. You were more than that."

"He was more than that to me. He'll always be my first kiss, the first guy I cared for, my first heartbreak. I hope he knows how much he meant to me. I hope he will look back when he's ninety and think of me with fondness. I hope one day, I'll be able to get over him and to find someone to love me the way he loves Trish."

"Ness..." Emmet said softly.

"Please, Emmet," she replied firmly. "Let it go. It's ridiculous to think anything could have come from it. We only met a few days ago."

"Sometimes a few days is all it takes," Emmet answered.

"I don't believe in love at first sight. I should say, I never *before* believed in love at first sight. Then I met Sean." She turned to look at him and took a deep breath. "You have been the best of friends to me but I just can't. I need to go home."

"Stay with me," Emmet begged. "Just a little longer."

"I can't, Emmet, I hope you understand why."

"More than you know," he replied.

"What now? Can you show me more?" She forced a smiled.

"Aye, I'll show you more, love. Let's eat."

She followed him into the cafeteria and said nothing as they waited in line. Emmet took her hand in his as the words to Keera's last text filled his thoughts.

Keera: They're going through with it… That bitch! She's lying to him! She hasn't told him anything. He's down on his knees asking for forgiveness while she's standing there, large as bloody life crying and saying he never loved her. All why Innis is throwing back whiskies. Where are you, Emmet? I might need you for some heavy lifting and an alibi if I have to kill her.

Chapter

Twenty-Six

"Trish, you can't be serious," Innis announced as he walked into the guest room.

"I'm perfectly serious, Innis," she answered packing up her things.

"You're actually going through with it?" He demanded. "That was your one chance of cutting it off, for us."

She let out an angry growl. "There is no us!" she hissed. "Sean is mine. That little tramp is not getting her claws into him any further."

"You're going through with the wedding because you don't want her to have him?" Innis was gobsmacked.

"He's mine," she said harshly.

"You are *mine*!" he replied.

"I *belong* to no one," she yanked her arm out of his grasp. "Especially not you." She headed to the door.

"I love you," Innis said.

She whirled around to face him.

"There, I've said it," he replied. "No strings, no what-ifs, no threats of exposure, just the truth. I can't stand beside my brother Saturday and watch you marry him because I love you."

"You're an eejit," she finally said as she walked out.

"Trish, please don't do this!" Innis begged. Heading out right behind her, he came face to face with his father. "Da'," he said tightly. Orin's eyes were cold, and his jaw was set.

"Innis," his father replied. "We need to talk, lad. Come with me."

Innis took a deep breath and followed his father out the front door and toward the boatshed. His eyes drifted to Sean helping Trish into Ole Bess. Trish didn't look up at him and that made Innis's chest ache. Cabhan stood at his Land Rover, his arms resting through the rolled down window of his open door.

"Bad luck, Inn," Cabhan said snidely.

"Lay off," Innis replied. Then, realizing what he said, continued with, "I don't know what you're talking about."

At the last minute, he heard Trish complain. "Why can't we go in Cabhan's car? It's a lot nicer than this old bag of bones."

Innis didn't hear Sean's response as he stepped into his father's boat shed. He knew Sean was going to be miserable married to her. More importantly to Innis, Trish was going to hate every second of being married to Sean. She needed Innis as much as he needed her.

"Innis," his father's voice brought him back to reality. Deirdre came out of the shadows and crossed her arms over her chest staring at him. A look of disapproval on her face.

"How long have you been sleeping with your brother's fiancée?" Orin demanded. Innis swallowed hard.

"I don't think I can do this," Ness said as she and Emmet waited in the lobby of the Plaza Hotel for Cabhan and Keera.

"They'll be staying at her parent's place, you'll not see them," Emmet replied. "You wanted to see Dublin, didn't you?"

"Not with *them*, Emmet," she whispered. "Not like this. I know he told her about me."

"Ness, trust me, you are part of this family now. You will be fine. You are truly remarkable," he said.

"Thank you," she answered. "But that's not the point."

"Leaving already?" they heard behind them. Turning, Paddy walked up. "Was your stay satisfying?"

"Paddy," Emmet warned.

"I do hope so. We pride ourselves on the... efficiency of our staff current or former," he went on ignoring Emmet's warning.

"Don't be an arse," Emmet went on.

"I'm not trying to be, Em," Paddy grinned. "I just wanted to make sure this lovely young lady had a wonderful time."

"I know exactly what you're doing," Emmet countered.

"Thank you, Paddy," Ness started. "I had a very satisfying stay here. And everything was... beyond expectations."

"I'm very glad to hear it," Paddy replied, his eyes flared as his smirk grew. "Don't be a stranger. I'm here most days, so if you'd like to be shown a real Irishman, you just let me know."

"All right, that does it," Emmet replied grasping Ness's arm. "We're leaving." Paddy grinned as they walked out of the lobby. "Ach, sorry about that, darlin'," Emmet said. "Paddy is my best friend but he's a chancer. Steer clear, aye?"

"He's kinda funny," Ness replied. "In a roguish sort of way."

"I wouldn't want any sister of mine with him," Emmet said.

"You have to admit he's handsome," Ness replied.

"Bah," Emmet scoffed. "Ah, there's Cabhan's car."

As a Land Rover pulled up, Cabhan and Keera greeted them.

"*Mora duit ar maidin*," Cabhan called.

"Good morning to you as well," Emmet smiled back.

"Hi," Ness replied.

"So, are ya ready to see the most beautiful city in all the world, Ness?" Cabhan asked.

"Absolutely," Ness replied sliding in next to Keera. "Bring on the rocky road to Dublin."

"Ha! Ya heard the song, did ya?" Cabhan asked.

"They played it last night in the pub," Ness revealed.

"Well, lucky for us, they've paved the road now," Cabhan winked.

"We've rooms at St. Helen. You'll love it," Keera said.

"I'm sure I will," Ness replied.

"I've packed you a few things," Keera said. "Although it looks like you survived two days of Emmet's fashion sense," she teased.

"He was amazing," she replied. "A wonderful friend and even attempted to be my wingman when this pretty cute bartender started flirting with me."

"Ooh, details!" Keera said.

"You first," Ness smiled. "Anything happen with that guy you met at Sheehan's?"

"Uh oh, Cabh, I'm afraid we're in for some female banter," Emmet said.

"Aye, I'll put the game on," Cabhan grinned turning on the radio.

Chapter

Twenty-Seven

"We're almost to the city, love," Emmet whispered nudging Ness off his shoulder. Immediately, Ness sat up and looked out the window.

"Welcome to Dublin, Ness," Cabhan said looking at her in the rearview mirror.

Gazing out the window as they drove, Ness listened to Emmet as he pointed out important landmarks.

"Dublin Castle... Temple Bar... Trinity College which is Sean's and my *Alma Mater*... Oscar Wilde's statue on St. Stephen's Green... National Library... The American Embassy... Of course, that's the famous River Liffey... back that way is the Guinness Storehouse, the best Guinness in the world and St. Patrick's Cathedral..." Ness was wide eyed and silent as Emmet spoke. Even Keera's usually bored demeanor was lifted as she gazed out the window.

"Now take a look at that bridge, love," Emmet started, pointing to the bridge as they passed. "What does that look like to you?" She stared at it for a moment. "Tilt your head to the side. Now what do you see? I'll give you a clue... it's a musical instrument."

"A harp! It's a harp!" Ness squealed after a moment.

"That's right. The harp is the national instrument of Ireland," Cabhan explained.

"Can we stop and walk around?" Ness asked. "I really want to go see Trinity. Is Grafton Street near there?"

Emmet's eyebrows rose. "And how would you be knowing about Grafton Street?"

Ness bit her lower lip.

"The romance novel?" Emmet asked.

"Yeah," she admitted.

"Well, no worries, Grafton is actually right around the corner from Trinity," he laughed. "Innis has an apartment there."

"Hotel first?" Cabhan offered.

"Sounds good, Cabh," Emmet replied. "I could use a good hot shower, a whiskey, and a stretch."

Sean was miserable. Trish was making him miserable. If she complained about one more thing, he wasn't sure he could hold his tongue. Massaging his hand, sore from clenching the steering wheel all the way to Dublin, he hated himself for what he was becoming. Ness and Trish. Every fiber of his being screamed at him to go and apologize to Ness, call off the wedding, and sweep the American off her feet. But he did none of that. Instead, he had crushed her heart and left her alone.

Crashing at Trish's parent's house, across from St. Helen's Hotel, seemed like a grand idea a week ago. Now, to be that close to Ness and not being able to see her, was torture. The thought she hated him, no matter how rightly so, tormented him. Huffing, he fell on the bed and groaned.

"Sean," Dermott called to him at the door. Sean sat up and eyed his future father-in-law. "Come get a pint down at the local, lad?" Dermott asked. "Let's let the women to their work."

Sean watched him but eventually agreed and stood up. "I'd enjoy that. Let me change shirts?"

Dermott nodded and left the room. Sean pulled out a clean shirt and tugged it over his head. When he looked back to the doorway, he paused when he caught Trish's eye.

"You're going out with da'?" She asked.

"For a pint," he answered. She nodded slowly.

"At least I know da' will keep you away from any other young redheads that throw themselves at you," she spat.

Sean's entire body stiffened and with every ounce of control he had, he stopped himself from shaking.

"Yeah," he answered tightly. "Don't have any male strippers at your hen party."

She took a step forward. "You know I wouldn't do that," she answered smoothly. "I love you. I don't want to be with anyone else."

"Good, because I don't think I would be able to forgive you if you're lying to me." He watched her eyes go dark and the color drain from her face. But almost immediately a gentle smile lifted her lips.

"I'd never lie to you," she answered.

He rubbed her arms and kissing her quickly. "I'd better get going," he said.

Never before had her kiss made him gag. But he felt absolutely nothing. He should at least enjoy kissing the woman he was going to spend the rest of his life with. He used to enjoy it, at least he thought. But now...

"Everything all right?" Dermott asked as Sean walked out. Realizing he had seen Sean shaking his head, Sean forced a smiled and nodded. "Where would you like to go?" Dermott asked.

"I don't care," Sean answered. As long as alcohol was involved, he would be fine with anywhere.

"Temple Bar? Grafton Street? Where?" Dermott asked.

"Grafton," he answered.

"Good, was hoping you'd say that," Dermott replied. "Let's catch the bus."

St. Helen's was a beautiful hotel. The white brick façade complimented the yellow gold accents. As Ness followed the others down the hallway towards their rooms, she took in the elegance of the mahogany wood trim and the stunning chandelier.

"Will the wedding take place here?" she finally asked.

"No, just the welcome. The actually ceremony will be back in Kerry," Cabhan explained pocketing his ID and accepting the hotel keys.

"The welcome?" Ness asked.

"It's tradition for the bride and groom to welcome their guests with entertainment and food. Where better than Dublin? The rehearsal party will take place here in two days before the actual wedding. Then everyone will travel back to Kerry for the ceremony."

"Seems like a lot of trouble," Ness said.

"Oh, Trish never does anything small," Cabhan replied handing the keys to the others.

"So..." Emmet said as they walked down the hall to their rooms. "What would you like to do? Want to go see Trinity?"

"Maybe tomorrow? I'm kinda beat and would just like to go get some food and maybe a pint at Grafton Street," she said.

"Perfect," Cabhan smiled. "Give me ten minutes? I need to call Rachael and change shirts."

"Checking in with the wife, are ya?" Emmet teased.

"When is she coming down?" Keera asked.

"Tomorrow, the kids are staying with her parents," Cabhan answered as they stopped at their hotel room doors.

"Grand!" Keera cheered.

"Well, let's all clean up and then go to Grafton," Emmet offered unlocking his door.

Once she was alone, Ness went to her window and drew back the curtains. Her breath caught in her throat. Her view was of the front courtyard, the manicured lawn, the flowers, and the globe looking statue in the small pond.

When she left America, she never thought she would feel so at home in Ireland. She finally belonged somewhere. She could feel it in her bones. This was home.

A knock on her door pulled her attention. "Ready so soon?" she called. Opening the door, she froze in terror.

"Hello, Nessie," Tyler said.

A scream caught in her throat.

Chapter

Twenty-Eight

"What are you doing here?" Ness squeaked out.

"Aren't you going to invite me in?" Tyler grinned. "You know how hot it makes me to see that fear in your eyes."

Taking a deep breath, Ness had to do something. And she wasn't alone. "Emmet! Cabhan! Keera!" She screamed.

Tyler's eyes grew wide as a surge of relief coursed through her when she saw three doors open. Emmet locked eyes with her, then his face turned as hard as stone when he saw the fleeting figure running up the hallway.

"Cabhan, come on!" Emmet shouted as he took off after Tyler.

"What in the bloody hell is going on?" Cabhan demanded hanging up the phone and buttoning his shirt as he raced after his brother.

"Ness? Are you all right?" Keera rushed to her. Ness nodded. "What in the hell happened?" Keera asked.

"Kee, there's something I need to tell you," Ness said.

Ness had just finished relating the tale she had told Sean when there was a knock at the door and Emmet's voice rang out. "Keera, Ness it's Emmet."

Keera opened the door and stepped aside as her two cousins came into the room. Emmet locked eyes with Ness.

"Did you catch him?" Ness asked but she knew by the look in his eyes that they hadn't.

"We lost him, Ness," Emmet said. "I'm sorry."

"Would someone kindly tell me what's going on?" Cabhan asked.

Ness took a deep breath and nodded. "Yes, Cabhan, please you and Emmet sit."

"I'm running to the bar and getting us something to drink. Wine or whiskey?" Keera offered. "You need one, Ness. You shouldn't have to relive that."

"Thank you. Wine please, my stomach is already in knots."

"We can go get something to eat at Grafton after," Emmet offered.

"Be right back," Keera said and hurried out the door.

"I wanted to have a conversation with you, lad," Dermott said as they sat on stools at a bar on Grafton Street their pints in hand.

"What's on your mind, Dermott?" Sean asked taking a gulp of his Guinness.

"You and Trisha," he said.

"That seems to be on a lot of people's minds," Sean answered.

"I wanted to talk about this new girl in the picture… lad, I know how it can be. Now, I love my daughter, and you know there is nothing I wouldn't do for her, including shooting you if need be. But with that said, I know what kind of woman she is and how she can be. I want you to be completely honest with me, Sean," he took a breath. "Can you live with her for the rest of your life? Trust me when I say marriage is tough enough. Brenda and I have seen some rough spots," he broke off for a moment then continued. "But we have the love of each other to help us through anything. We emerge stronger through the fire by going in together. We both have faults, but it's how we handle them that builds trust, love, and a strong marriage. So, I ask you, Sean… do you love my daughter more than anything or *anyone* else?"

Sean was staring into the froth of his beer. He didn't know his own heart and mind.

"Dermott," he started. "I…"

"I thought so," he cut him off. "Sean, you can't hide it from a man who has been married for nearly thirty years."

Sean wished he could get answers from the milky darkness. But then, like a jackal, the hair on the back of his neck stood on end. Turning to see what could have caused it, he locked eyes with a green meadow in the face he would know anywhere. His chest tightened, his breath caught, his heart pounded. Ness stood in the doorway of the pub staring at him. God, he had missed her.

Dermott watched Sean as he looked at the young woman by the door. He knew Sean had never looked at Trish like that. Sean was head over heels for Ness even in the short time they knew each other. Dermott's eyes followed Sean's, his chest constricting. *That* was what was so familiar about her when he had seen Ness the other night. Brenda was right. *My god, it's like looking into the past, except the eyes are wrong. No, not wrong just different. Bren's was right... Ness did have her father's eyes. My god, she is stunning, just like her mother,* Dermott thought.

Chapter

Twenty-Nine

Ness's eyes were drawn almost instinctively to the bar. Sean sat with the same man she had seen back in Killarney. The memory of that night made it hard for her to concentrate. Used to adrenaline causing such a reaction, Ness was not prepared for the tears that threatened. Sean was staring at her with a look she could not describe. Was he angry she was there? Her pride flared telling her she had every right to be there as he did. Or was he upset that his brothers were helping her? She could not force his family to choose. It was unfair of her to cause a divide.

"Why don't you go have a beer with Sean?" she forced a smile. "I'll walk around for a bit and enjoy the music." Strains of a live band playing down the road reached their ears.

"Oh no, girl, you're not getting away from us and I don't want you to be thinking we're choosing sides… Sean is my brother but he's being an eejit at the moment and you are our guest. You are not safe by yourself. So no, I'm not letting you out of my sight."

"I agree," Keera voiced. "Besides, that maniac is still out there. From now on you don't go anywhere alone. Not even to the toilets."

"Ness," Cabhan stepped towards her. "We're not choosing sides, Emmet is right."

"I'm sorry what?" Emmet teased. "What did you say?"

"Lay off," Cabhan replied. "Sean will always be our brother and we will always love him but right now we need to make sure you're safe."

"Thank you," Ness said.

"So, what are we gonna do?" Keera asked.

"I want a beer and then I want to go looking around, maybe a little tourist shopping," Ness replied. "Get my mind off everything."

"Would you like to go somewhere else? Thing about Ireland is there are more pubs than houses," Emmet replied.

"No," she said. "I've let a man dictate my entire life so far. This is supposed to be a new beginning for me, and I'll not let a man rule me again."

"There's no sense in torturing yourself," Cabhan reasoned.

"I will not let him or my feelings for him dictate where I can and cannot go. I have to conquer this. I have to prove there is room on this island for the both of us. Now... *please* let me buy us a round."

"Well, I suppose we can allow that since you asked so nicely," Emmet said. "Mine's a pint of the black stuff."

"Guinness," Keera supplied.

"Ha," she laughed. "Oh, I know. I've heard him order it the last couple days. Cabhan, what would you like?"

"Same," Cabhan replied.

"Kee?"

"I'll take a Bulmers," Keera supplied, her phone buzzing in her hand. She grinned as she read the text.

Ness confirmed and walked straight up to the bar.

"Good afternoon, Sean," she forced a smile. "It's a lovely day. And you must be Trish's father. I want to apologize for how we met a few days ago."

"Could I get you a refill?" Ness asked Dermott indicating his empty glass. Before he could reply, she called the bartender over. "Another one of those," she said pointing to the glass. "And three pints of Guinness and one... Bulmers? Is it?" The bartender nodded and started pouring the drinks. "Sean, I'm sorry, did you want another? You still have half a pint, so I didn't think to ask."

"Thanks," he muttered. "But no."

"Okay," she answered with a wide, breathtaking grin.

Dermott had to stop himself from laughing. *Just like her mother*, he thought.

"Is this your first time in Ireland, Ness?" he asked.

She nodded. "It's lovely," she replied. "I'm very excited to see as much as I can before going back home."

Dermott saw the very visible flinch from Sean. "Then you should join us on the barge tonight for a little get together dinner and music. There's no better way to see this grand old city," Dermott invited.

"Oh, um... I don't think that would be-" she began.

"Please," Dermott interrupted. "It's going to be a lovely time and a good friend of mine is going to be providing live music while we eat. It's part of the welcome. You'll be my guest."

"Well... um," her eyes unconsciously drifted toward Sean. Luckily, she was saved from saying anything by the bartender coming back to her.

Ness counted out the money and handed it to him.

The barman gave her the beers with a flirtatious wink. She grinned back and bit her lower lip as she looked at him. Dermott watched Sean bristle when he saw the exchange.

"Of course, you're welcome to bring a date to the event tonight," Dermott said eyeing the man behind the bar.

Ness laughed. "It does sound like fun. Are you sure Trish won't mind?"

"I'll make sure of it," he answered.

"I'd like that. Thank you," Ness said. "Please enjoy your beer."

"Cheers," he smiled. "It's good to meet you Nessa."

"And you, Mr. Riley," she took the drinks and headed toward the table Emmet had found.

"Why did you do that?" Sean whispered harshly. "You know Trish will not be happy. And I'll get the brunt of it."

"I'll deal with my daughter," Dermott answered. "Go to your family, Sean."

"This isn't helping the situation, Dermott," Sean

grumbled as he slid off his stool and walked away.

"Oh, on the contrary," Dermott replied to himself. "I think it's helping quite a bit."

Chapter

Thirty

"You did what?" Trish demanded from her father.

"I invited Nessa to the festivities tonight," Dermott repeated.

"Dermott," Brenda breathed. "Why?"

"Because I think it's high time we all know the truth, Bren," he replied locking eyes with his wife.

"How could you betray me like that?" Trish demanded.

"I have not betrayed you anymore than you have betrayed Sean with Innis," Dermott said.

Trish paled. "You don't know what you're talking about."

"Don't I?" Dermott questioned. "Love, I am your father

and I'm a man. I've seen the looks between you two and last weekend when you and Innis were here making final preparations, you didn't come home. I know you're saving money so you wouldn't have wasted it on a hotel. You stayed with Innis at his flat on Grafton."

"I — he slept on the couch," she stuttered.

"You can't lie to me, love," Dermott scoffed. "You two slept together, it's plainly obvious. We love you no matter what, but you've lied to Sean. He is a good and honorable man who has found someone he feels more for, just like you and Innis. How can you deny him that?"

"So, you are punishing me for a mistake?" Trish cried as tears rolled down her cheeks.

"I'm not punishing you, love," he said.

"You betrayed me, Da'," she rebuttaled. "You betrayed me by inviting that slapper to my wedding welcome."

"Watch your language," Dermott scolded when he saw his wife flinch and tears well in her eyes.

"I'll say whatever the hell I want to say," she yelled. "You're stealing my future!"

"I'm giving you your happiness," Dermott said. "I know you love Innis and you are simply using Sean. I want you to be happy." Then, gazing at his wife, he went on. "A happiness I have had every day since I married your mother. No matter what."

Brenda burst into tears and rushed out of the room. Dermott looked at his daughter.

"I love your mother," Dermott said. "Can you honestly look at me and tell me you love Sean? Love him enough to spend the rest of your life with him? To have his children? Through thick and thin, no matter what?"

Trish furiously wiped the tears running down her cheeks as she clutched her arms around her waist.

"Please, Daddy," she said.

"What is it, girl? You know you can tell me anything," Dermott replied.

"Please, I want to marry him," she answered.

"Why?"

"I... I have to," she answered.

Dermott eyed his daughter as realization came over him. "Oh jaysus, Trish," he breathed.

"Come on," Keera begged Ness over the hotel phone.

"No, Keera," Ness replied. "I don't know why Mr. Riley invited me but I won't do that to Sean, Trish, or myself."

"What about me or Emmet?" Keera asked. "'Cause if you stay behind, one of us will have to stay with you."

"I don't ask either of you to stay with me," Ness replied.

"No, but you know one of us will, especially with that gobshite still out there," Keera was saying. "You're forcing one of us not to go."

"You're not playing fair," Ness sighed.

"Of course I'm not playing fair, I'm your friend," Keera replied.

"Emmet would've played fair," Ness said.

"I wouldn't count on it," she answered. "Come on! You're my best friend, you *can't* leave me alone with all those old folks."

Again, Ness sighed, harsher this time. "You owe me big time," she finally conceded.

Keera squealed. "And I swear to pay up," she promised.

"What's the dress code?"

"Oh," Keera replied. "I forgot... it's semi-formal."

"Kee, I don't have a little black dress."

"We are in the biggest city in Ireland," Keera answered. "There's shops galore."

"Fine," Ness replied. "I've learned never to argue with you O'Quinns."

Chapter

Thirty-One

Sean couldn't stop the bounce of his knee as he waited for his whiskey. The former Guinness barge canal cruise for his wedding welcome should have been the thing he was looking forward to the most. Instead, the walls were closing in and he felt claustrophobic waiting for Ness to arrive.

"Everything all right, lad?" his father's voice behind him made him jump.

"Fine," his voice was higher than it had been since he was thirteen years old.

"What is it, son?" Orin asked ordering a beer and a glass of wine for Deirdre.

"Dermott invited Ness here tonight," Sean spilled.

"Why would he do that?"

"I don't know."

He heard Dermott's voice outside the barge just as the bartender handed over the whiskey. Taking it, he shot it down in one swallow. Trish, Brenda, and Dermott walked down the steps and into the belly of the barge. Sean forced a smile, but he was starting to panic.

Trish's gaze found Innis's and Sean swore he saw tears gather in her eyes. Sean's fist clenched but he went to his fiancée and forced himself to kiss her. She smiled at him and for a moment he felt the same thing he'd felt for the years they had been friends. She was a wonderful friend and he knew he could love her if he just let it happen. Tenderly, he caressed her cheek and smiled when she leaned into his touch. Out of the corner of his eye, Sean saw Innis push passed everyone and go above deck. A second later the smell of Innis's favorite cigarettes wafted towards them.

Odd, he thought. Innis never smoked in front of the family. Their stepmother would never allow it, and Emmet would hate it.

"Can I get you something to drink?" Sean asked her.

"A water," she replied.

"Sure? You don't want a wine?" he asked. She shook her head and looked down. "All right," he smiled. "Go on in and sit down, love."

"Sean…" she started. "I…"

"What is it?" he asked gently.

"I – ehm," she started again. "I love you."

"I love you, too."

"Do you?"

"Of course, now, let me take care of you."

Trish took her seat at the table set for two, bedecked in bride and groom decorations as Sean turned back to her parents.

"Brenda, Dermott," he nodded to them.

"Sean," Brenda answered. "You look very handsome."

"Thank you," he replied. "And you look lovely. I want to apologize for what happened. I have no explanation for it, but I hope you will not hold it against me."

"Sean, I do know what forbidden love is like," she said softly. "I would never want those I love to judge me for my past," she took Dermott's hand. "As long as I have your word you will never hurt my daughter, all is well between us."

"I swear to you, Brenda, I only want to make Trish happy," Sean said.

She smiled at him and took her leave to say hello to Sean's mother.

"Dermott," Sean called to him before he could follow his wife to the lower deck. "Is everything all right?"

"I believe it will be, Sean," Dermott replied.

The barge would cast off in under fifteen minutes and after handing Trish her water, Sean stepped out up to the top deck. Innis greedily drew on his cigarette, removing the tobacco from his lips and puffing out the smoke when he saw Sean.

"Thank you for coming tonight, Innis," Sean said.

His brother nodded as he pulled on his cigarette again clearly not in the mood to talk to anyone.

"Are you all right?" Sean asked.

"I'm fine, Sean," Innis answered.

"It's just... well, I haven't seen you like this before," Sean said.

"And how exactly am I?" Innis hissed blowing the smoke out of the corner of his mouth away from his brother.

"You just seem to have something preying on your mind, that's all."

"Maybe I do," he answered looking out across the canal and throwing his spent cigarette into the water. "Go on back to your guests, Sean. I'll be fine."

"They will want the best man too," Sean smiled.

Innis closed his eyes and took a deep breath. Pulling out his cigarette pack, he tapped out another one, lit it, and took a long draw.

"I'll be there in a minute," he answered.

"Are you sure there's nothing wrong?" Sean asked. His brother looked like he wanted to jump into the water.

"Oh, Christ Almighty, Sean just leave me be!" Innis shouted. Sean took a startled step back.

"Sorry," he mumbled and headed back inside.

"What was that about?" Orin asked standing at the bar, getting a drink for Dermott.

"I am not entirely certain," Sean replied. "I think he has something on his mind."

"Well, whatever it is, don't let his sour mood bother you," Orin said.

"Has he said anything to you?"

"Sometimes a father knows his children better than they know themselves," Orin said cryptically.

"All right," Sean breathed out. "I'll pretend like I

understood that."

"Sean!" A young female voice cried. Sean turned to the belly of the barge and grinned.

"Sinéad!" He cried. His sister raced to him and was engulfed in his arms. "I didn't know you'd be able to make it!"

"Oh, don't be silly!" she laughed. "Of course, I was going to make it. Cabhan picked me up from the airport earlier." Sean looked around and caught his eldest brother's eye.

"Thank you," he mouthed. Cabhan winked. "It's good to see you, darlin'," Sean turned back to their sister. "You look fine!"

"So do you," she grinned. "How are you?"

"I've missed ya," he said. "How's Australia?"

"Beautiful! But glad to be back. How are things here?"

"Just busy."

"I'm so happy for you!" Sinéad gushed rubbing her hand up and down his arm.

"Sinéad," her mother called. "Come on over, love. I want you to meet someone."

"Coming, mum," she replied then turned back to Sean. "Catch up? Drinks at Temple Bar?"

"Grand idea," Sean answered. His baby sister, Deirdre's and Orin's daughter, came into the world when he was still a boy. At nineteen, she was growing into a rather beautiful young woman and Sean knew he and his brothers would have their work cut out for them keeping all the rogues away from her.

Smiling as he watched her laugh at something their da' said, Sean's eyes drifted to the entry as a pair of black strappy high heels followed by a pair of silky alabaster legs stepped down into the barge. He blinked as his eyes kept trailing up. Thin black silk cut at all angles at the hem, a waist accentuated by a black silk sash and a square neckline where he recognized a silver Claddagh necklace hanging around an alabaster neck, greeted him. Spaghetti straps held the dress in place and red hair was swept up, hanging in tendrils at Ness's neck. Sean's eyes froze on an upturned pair of pink lips then his eyes found the green meadows sparkling with mischief and laughter gazing back at Emmet coming in behind her.

The moment her eyes locked with his, her bright smile faltered and with it, his resolve.

Sean looked so handsome in his white oxford shirt, unbuttoned at the collar. Sport coat and black slacks paired well with black converse shoes. His hair was trimmed, and his face looked smooth.

"Ness," she heard Deirdre call to her.

Breaking eye contact with Sean, she sought out his mother. Deirdre stood with Trish's parents in the middle of the barge. Dermott gave her a friendly smile, but Brenda looked as if she had been struck by lightning.

Emmet placed a hand on her back and went to get them a drink.

"Glad you could make it, dear," Dermott said.

"Yes indeed," Deirdre smiled widely at her. "It's good to see you again. You look lovely."

"Thank you," Ness replied.

"This is my daughter Sinéad," Deirdre introduced the

young woman beside her.

"Nice to meet you," Ness said.

"And you," Sinéad replied, wide eyes and a genuine smile lent to her youthful look.

"Ness, allow me introduce my wife Brenda," Dermott said indicating the woman beside him white-knuckling her glass of wine.

"Hi," Ness replied then corrected herself. "A pleasure, Mrs. Riley."

Brenda shook herself out of her stupor and tried to smile.

"Likewise," she answered tightly.

Saved from Brenda's odd stare by Emmet handing her a glass of wine, Ness immediately took him up on his offer of going up to the top deck.

Throughout the evening, the bride and groom were wished well with toasts, gifts, and cheers. But no matter how fervent Ness tried not to look at Sean, their eyes locked more often than not. Sinéad, who sat on the opposite side of Emmet, tapped his shoulder when Ness excused herself to go above deck.

"You, Em, have been keeping secrets," Sinéad whispered.

"Hmm?" he asked.

"What did I miss between those two?"

"Oh, love, far too much."

"You're gonna have to explain," she begged. Emmet

smirked. "And what about those two?"

Emmet's eyes turned to Trish and Innis who had locked eyes yet again. Licking his lips in deliberation, Emmet shrugged.

"No proof," he whispered.

"But..." Sinéad pressed.

"Affair," Emmet mouthed.

"No!" Sinéad gasped.

"A couple of us have seen them kissing pretty heatedly," Emmet explained.

"How could he?" She breathed looking at Innis.

"The heart wants what the heart wants, come on, Miss Psychology Major," Emmet teased.

"You and I are going to have a drink tonight and you're gonna fill me in on all the latest that I've missed," she said.

"I'm meeting Ness at the bar for a drink tonight, I'll text you when she goes to her room," Emmet said.

"Is there something going on with you two?" Sinéad asked confused.

Emmet looked over at her surprised.

"Saints, no," he replied chuckling.

"Well you can't blame me for wondering," she said. "You two seem so... close."

"I'm protecting her, Fee," Emmet replied. Her brows furrowed deeply. "All will be explained tonight."

"Better be," she answered.

Chapter

Thirty-Two

The evening passed without much excitement. Dermott's friend sang and played the guitar at one end of the barge during the ride. Several people went above deck to take in the passing city and some fresh air. Ness found it fascinating to watch the barge stop at the canal locks and to see the captain maneuver the boat through them.

Night fell quickly and the barge was lit with Christmas lights strung around the top. Going above deck for a breath of fresh air, Ness watched the buildings pass by but then suddenly realized she wasn't alone; Sean sat on one of the benches.

"Oh," she jumped. "I'm sorry."

"No, it's fine," he said softly. "Don't go."

"I just came up for some air, it's a little stuffy in there," she replied wrapping her arms around herself, suddenly feeling the chill in the air.

"You must be freezing," he said walking over to her and draping his blazer around her shoulders. She sank deeper into its warmth.

"Thanks," she answered. "The dress was Keera's choice."

"You look stunning," Sean said softly.

"Thank you," she answered turning away from him to watch the city.

"I've missed you," he finally said. She looked back at him, her eyes searched his. "I've been the worst of fools, Ness," he went on. "I just... I don't know which way is up anymore."

"You don't have to say anything, Sean," Ness stopped him.

"But I do," he said. "I've hurt you and I am so unbelievably sorry. If I could take it back, do things differently, I would. Had I known I was your first kiss, I would never have..." he broke off, sighed, and thrust his hands into his suit pants pockets.

"You would never have what?" Ness pressed. "Kissed me?"

"Stolen that bit of innocence from you," he admitted.

"Sean, I'm twenty-two, it's high time I'm kissed. I have no regrets."

"I do," he sighed.

"Oh," she answered as her face paled and her breath left her in one short woosh. "That's different, then. I'm sorry. I didn't realize."

She turned to go but Sean grabbed her arm and pulled

her into him. His lips were on hers before she knew what was going on.

"My regret, Ness," he whispered pulling away slightly. "Is that I can't do *that* every moment of every day. I regret I cannot love you the way I want to love you. I regret I have to stop myself every time because I don't want to stop. I want to make love to you. I want to make you mine. I want forever with you."

"I feel the same, Sean," she said her breath hitching. "But we hardly know each other."

"When you know you know. And I know. I want to be your champion. I want to protect you from your darkest fears. I want you to want me."

"I do want you. But I want you to want me too," she said.

"I do," he said. His eyes tightened but he was silent. Finally, the tune to the song *Carrickfergus* reached their ears. Slow and steady.

"Dance with me," he said softly. "Please, just one song."

"Yes," she acquiesced.

He slipped his arms around her waist, pulled her to him and slowly they began rocking to the music. It wasn't easy considering the place they danced was not more than two feet wide. But she didn't care. Alone, pressed against each other, moving as one to the slow rhythm of the music. Their eyes closed, they breathed as one.

When the music eventually ended, Sean did not pull away.

"Ness, I'm so sorry," he whispered into her hair.

"I've fallen in love with you, Sean," she admitted.

Sean's entire body stiffened. Then realizing what she just said, Ness took two steps back, breaking their embrace and tripping on a loose floorboard.

"Whoa," Emmet smiled catching her as he came up the steps. "Easy love, I know I'm easy to fall for but try not to hurt yourself," he winked.

"Sorry," she said going back to her seat but not before hearing Emmet speak with Sean.

"Everyone's wondering where you are. It's time for the champagne toast."

Ness reached her seat and took a long gulp of her water. Calming her breathing, she tried to focus on anything but Sean. Her face was burning up and she was sure she was flushed. Looking down, she realized she still wore Sean's suit jacket. Shrugging out of it quickly, she saw someone in her peripheral sit in Emmet's chair. Raising her gaze, she was shocked and a little horrified when she saw Brenda, Trish's mother beside her.

"Are you all right?" Brenda asked gently. Ness stared at her.

"I'm fine, thank you," she answered.

"Is there anything I can do to help you?" Brenda asked.

Ness pulled her brows together. "Why would you want to help me?"

Brenda flinched slightly. "I know how things can be," she started softly. "But trust me when I say all will turn out for the best. It may not be what you want, but it will turn out for the best."

Ness didn't know why the woman's words comforted her or why she couldn't help the small smile that lifted her lips.

"You are so lovely, my dear," Brenda said softly raising her hand to Ness's cheek.

Ness instinctively pulled away from Brenda's touch, uncertain if it was meant as a friend or foe. Her eyes drifted to Trish sitting at the bride's table looking pale and green. Trish had her arms wrapped around herself as if she was sick. Brenda followed her gaze.

"Trish has not been feeling well. It has nothing to do with you," Brenda said. "It's nerves that's all."

Ness said nothing but seeing Emmet and Sean return, she averted her eyes as Sean walked past them. Brenda stood and went back to her own seat.

"We're about to dock, love," Emmet said as Ness yawned. "And from the look of it, you could use your bed."

"Sorry," she said. "It's the wine."

"Well, maybe you'll join me for another glass in the hotel bar?" Emmet asked.

"You drink wine?" She asked.

"Ehm, no," Emmet answered. "Never touch the stuff meself. But I'll have a whiskey, you can have the wine."

Chapter

Thirty-Three

Tyler struck the steering wheel of his rental car as he watched Ness get into Emmet's car at the canal docks. Having paid one of the waiters on the barge, Tyler knew where they would dock and waited for them. He hadn't expected Ness to be able to call out back at St. Helen's or Emmet to nearly catch him. A man that size should not be so quick on his feet.

The original plan needed to be modified. Tyler had to find a way to get Ness away from anyone else. He decided to take a step back and wait for the perfect moment. They had to leave her unguarded sometime and when they did, he would be ready.

Trish looked up to see her dance instructor, Placido waltz into the room. The flamboyant Italian grinned at her and rushed over.

"Trisha, *bella mia!*" he called. "How are you today?"

"Hiya, Placido," she smiled sadly as she reached for her right foot and stretched.

"Oh, Trisha," he knelt down to be eye level with her. "You should be happy. 'Tis the eve of your wedding!"

"Just a lot on my mind," she answered.

"And where is your groom?" he asked.

"Present and accounted for," Sean's voice came from the door. Trish and Placido looked over to see Sean walk in, carrying a duffle bag. "But I'm gonna need to change," Sean said.

"Hurry hurry," Placido said. "We have very little time to make you two perfect."

"Won't be a second," he answered and headed to the locker rooms. Only then did Trish see Innis standing by the door and the blood drained from her face.

"What the hell are you doing here?" she hissed when they were relatively alone.

"It wasn't my choice, was it?" he replied. "Sean thought I should join you for the last session since I'll be dancing as well."

"I don't want you here," she said.

"I can't help that, love."

"I want you to leave."

"Giving what excuse?"

"I don't care."

"Trish, look," he sighed. "I'm here for you and my

brother."

"I don't want you here," she said again.

"I heard you the first time, love."

She huffed off onto the dance floor. Innis watched her go. She thought she would be sick and not just because of the main reason which she refused to even voice yet. Hating the fear, anxiety, and guilt rolling around her heart and mind, Trish tried to focus on what she was about to do. Always a dancer since she was little, she loved the idea of putting on a show for her first dance with her husband. But Sean was no dancer and they always had difficulty molding well on the dancefloor.

Hearing the door open, she turned to see Sean emerge in male dance sweats and a t-shirt, typing on his phone. He looked up and briefly smiled at Innis before sliding his phone into a pocket of the duffle and setting the bag down by the chairs.

"Good," Placido called seeing Sean was ready. "Take your fiancée and let's dance!"

The music started and Sean offered his hand to her. Pulling her into him, they began the choreography.

An hour and two water bottles later, Trish and Sean had sweat dripping down their faces and Sean's grey t-shirt had a very visible sweat *V* on the front. But Innis couldn't take his eyes off of Trish. She was made to dance. Watching her in his brother's arms, wrapped around his body, Innis felt a sudden sense of possession and jealously course through him.

"No, no, no," Placido shook his head breaking Innis's concentration. Sean and Trish split and looked at their dance instructor. Sean wiped the sweat off his forehead with the edge of his shirt. "Sean, you need to take more control. You are the man. You bring her into you," Placido demonstrated by yanking Trish into him. "And you make love to her on the dance floor. This is the dance of passion. The tango is a man's dance. She will do what you want her to do because you command it." His words were pronounced as he demonstrated by swinging Trish around. "Now, try it again."

Sean sighed but drew Trish into him. The music started and they began to dance. They hadn't gotten to the fifth step before Placido stopped them.

"You," he called to Innis. "Come here."

"Oh no," Innis replied. "I'm just here to watch."

"I need another man," Placido said impatiently. "Come here." His tone left little room to argue. Innis stood and headed over. "Sean, watch," Placido replied. He took Innis's hand and placed it on Trish's lower back. The look in her eye screamed at him. "Now, you two, dance."

The music started and Innis knew this would be the last time he would have her in his arms. Pulling her into him, he took control. Though he felt the slight resistance in her body at first, she soon followed his lead. Closing his eyes, he breathed her in. Listening to the music, Innis let the rhythm guide him. At first it was a simple sway back and forth, then the music picked up its pace and Innis pushed her away from him holding on to her wrist. Pulling her back, he lifted her leg and hooked it around his hip as they rocked back and forth, his fingers feathered up her bare leg to the edge of her spandex shorts. Then suddenly he twirled her around and she slid down through his legs holding onto his thigh.

Pulling her back up to him, Innis lifted her and swung her around with him. Dramatically dropping her hands, only grasping the back of her neck in a powerful command, Innis walked her across the dance floor continuing with the movements of *slow – slow – quick, quick – slow*.

She gazed into his eyes and flicked her leg out around his and hooked around his knee as he dragged her backwards. Innis stood tall as she slid into him and pulled her up, holding her flush. His hand gripped her backside and pressed their hips together. Again, they rocked together. She pushed away, but he caught her hand and twirled her around, pulling her back.

When the music came to an end, he dipped her nearly to the floor caressing the side of her body from ankle to shoulder in a sensual touch. His head dipped down between her breasts as she arched her back against his hold and ran her fingers through his hair.

The entire room was silent. Eventually he lifted her to be level with him and felt her lips gently brush his. Both were breathing heavily, their hearts pounded as one. All he wanted to do was take her back to his flat and make her his again. They gazed into each other eyes for a long moment.

"*Bravi*!" Placido cried clapping his hands wildly. "*Bravi tutti*! Brilliant! Absolutely brilliant! Oh, where did you study? You have such natural talent!"

Reluctantly, Innis broke away from her and turned to the dance instructor.

"I've ehm… never danced the tango before in my life," he said. "That was the first time."

"Such passion!" he cried. "You must let me train you. You could be a big star."

"Eh… no," Innis answered.

"I must have you in my school! See, Sean?" Placido said. "That is the kind of passion you must have when dancing the tango. *Bravi!*"

Sean stood at the edge of the dance floor, arms crossed, staring at them. Slowly, Trish walked over to him and forced a smile. Sean said nothing as he stared at her. Innis resumed his seat by the door.

"How long?" Sean's voice was low and raw.

"What?" Trish asked.

"How long has this been going on between you two?"

"What do you mean?"

Without another word, Sean turned and stalked out the door. Trish locked eyes with Innis for a moment, then raced after Sean.

"Sean! Wait!" she cried. She caught up with him outside and grabbed his arm. "Sean!"

"What the hell was that about, Trish?" Sean demanded as he whirled around. Pedestrians gawked. "You've never danced like that with me. You've never even *looked* at me like that. He touched you in a way *I* don't even touch you."

"It was part of the dance," she reasoned.

"Don't lie to me anymore!" Sean shouted. "Are you sleeping with him?"

"Sean..." she breathed.

"Answer me!" he yelled. She flinched and closed her eyes. "Have you slept with him?" he bit out. She curled her lips around her teeth but nodded. Sean was quiet. "How long?" He whispered, pain evident in his voice.

She finally looked up at him and he saw the answer in her eyes. God, he wanted to punch something, mostly, his brother.

"How could you do this to me?" he demanded.

"I'm so sorry," she said taking a step forward towards him.

"He's my brother!" Sean shouted. "You lied to me! You made me feel like the lowest and most horrible person in the world and all along you were laughing behind my back and sleeping with my brother! Gah!" he screamed, turning away from her and thrusting his hands through his hair.

"Is everything all right, here?" A policeman walked up. "Miss, is this man bothering you?" he asked Trish.

She shook her head. "He's my fiancé," she said.

"Ha! No, I'm not. Not anymore," Sean spat, walking away from her.

"Sean, please!" she yelled after him.

"Don't Trish," he turned back. "Just don't. The wedding is off. I can't even look at you right now."

"Sean!" She cried his name but he ignored her

Hearing the policeman ask if she was all right, and Innis's voice calling to her was the last thing Sean heard before he broke into a run. He was so close to going back and hitting his brother. That was a fight he wouldn't win, but he would feel better. The only thing he wanted was to get away. His legs pumped harder as he ran faster through the streets of Dublin. He had to get away.

Chapter

Thirty-Four

Something shrill startled Ness awake. Gasping, she sat straight up and looked around the room. Her phone was ringing on her nightstand. Reaching over, she read the name and answered.

"Sean?"

"Ness... it's Trish," Ness's stomach flipped. "I'm sorry to call, but I need your help."

"Is everything all right?" Ness asked swinging her legs over the edge of her bed and turning on the light.

"No," Trish sobbed. "Could you tell me if Sean's there with you?"

"What? No!" Ness cried.

"I'm sorry, I don't mean it like that," she said. "I just... oh god... he is so angry with me and I don't know where he is.

I've looked all around the city at all of our usual hangouts, and I can't find him."

"What happened?" Ness asked.

"We... oh god... we got into a huge fight," Trish began. "Please, if he is there and doesn't want me to know, could you just say yes? Don't tell him. I understand he doesn't want to talk to me, but I just need to make sure he's all right."

"Trish, he's not here. I'm not lying to you," she pledged.

"The last text he sent was to you," Trish said. "Apologizing for the other day."

Ness nodded. She had gotten his text but didn't know how to respond.

"If I hear from him or see him, I'll be sure to call you," Ness said.

"Thank you," Trish replied. "I'm sorry I've been so rude to you. I just... I see the love he has for you and I'm jealous. He's never looked at me like that."

"Look, I... I care about him," Ness started. "But he's marrying you. He's made his choice." Trish sobbed again. "I'll text his phone if I find him, okay?"

"Okay, thank you," Trish said before hanging up.

Ness dialed Emmet's number and waited.

"Hello?" Emmet's groggy voice answered after four rings.

"Em? It's Ness," she said.

"Are you all right?" He questioned sounding instantly awake.

"I'm fine," she answered. "But I just got a really weird

phone call. Trish called me on Sean's phone."

"Is he all right?" Emmet asked.

"She isn't sure," she explained. "Apparently they got into this huge fight earlier and he left his phone with her. She hasn't heard from him."

"Why would she call you?"

"She thought he was with me. Have you heard from him?"

"Hang on, let me check," he replied. "Yeah, I have a voice message. Let me call you back," Emmet hung up and Ness waited thinking about Sean's unexpected text from earlier that day.

She had been walking around Trinity College with Emmet waiting to see the Book of Kells, when her cell phone rang a notification.

Sean: Ness, I want to apologize for what happened on the barge. I've been fighting my attraction to you because I do not want to hurt Trish, but by denying it, I have hurt you. Please forgive me. I hope you at least know I would do anything to protect you.

At the time, Ness debated on responding and ended up pocketing her phone before she did. But as she waited in the muted light of her hotel room for Emmet's phone call, she wished she had replied. Gazing at the text again, she jumped when Emmet's picture showed up and her phone rang.

"Sean called me. He said he was all right and that he's in room forty-nine. It's down the hall. I'll go check on him," Emmet explained.

"Take your phone and call me," Ness asked. "I'll call Trish back."

"He asked me not to tell anyone where he was," Emmet confided.

"I won't," she answered. "But she needs to know he's okay. I'll just tell her you've heard from him. She'll be fine with that."

Emmet knocked on Sean's hotel door. A few moments later it opened, and Sean stood there looking drunk and mad as hell.

"Piss off," he muttered about to close the door. Emmet stopped him.

"Why don't you tell me what's going on? I brought whiskey," Emmet held up a fifth of whiskey he had stashed in his room.

Sean stared at it for a moment then opened the door wider so Emmet could come in. The room had been trashed.

"What the hell happened here?" Emmet asked looking around.

"I got angry, what do you think?" Sean demanded.

"I'm not the enemy," Emmet said closing the door. "Come sit down and tell me what happened."

Emmet produced two glasses and poured the whiskey as Sean sat on the bed.

"Women!" Sean finally snarled after tossing back the alcohol. "I can't understand them!"

"Who can?" Emmet asked sitting in the chair by the window.

Sean grabbed the bottle off the nightstand and poured himself a little more.

"I mean Ness can't stand the sight of me and Trish is sleeping with my brother," Sean said. Emmet didn't react and his silence drew Sean's attention. "Fantastic, so you knew? Jaysus, am I the only one who didn't?" Sean shouted.

"Tell me what happened, Sean. Talk to me."

Finally, Sean told him the whole story. Still sipping his first whiskey, Emmet grabbed the bottle before Sean could refill his glass again.

"God, Emmet you should have seen the way they danced. I've never been so turned on and so unbelievably angry at the same time."

"What are you wanting to do about tomorrow?"

"She lied to me! She slept with my brother when she promised me, she kept herself for me alone. I don't care that she's slept around before. But not with my brother!"

"Sean..." Emmet started.

"I have never been with a woman, Emmet," Sean admitted. "I have kept myself for my wife. I never wanted to look at her and think of another. I've felt this crushing guilt because of how I feel about Ness thinking how heartbroken Trish would be having kept herself for me and all the while she's shagging my brother!"

"Sean, it's commendable you want to keep yourself for your wife... a bit archaic but commendable," Emmet started. "The main question is, can you forgive her for lying to you? Accepting her faults can you, Sean, live with her or more importantly, live without her?"

"What do I do?" Sean asked.

"I can't answer that for you. The question you need to ask is will there be a wedding tomorrow?" Emmet asked.

Chapter

Thirty-Five

"I can't believe that eejit is going through with this after *everything*!" Keera was fuming.

Ness sat on the bed with a cup of tea, her legs curled under her. The news the wedding was still on came at around 5am that morning and Ness forced herself not to cry.

"Doesn't he know she's been lying to him and cheating on him by sleeping with anything in pants? Ugh, men I swear! I don't understand them!" Keera cried.

Sinéad nodded her agreement as she fixed her hair in the mirror. "I wonder if he's only doing this as some measuring contest with Innis."

"Wouldn't surprise me," Keera grumbled. Then catching Ness's eye in the mirror, her face softened. "I am so sorry, honey." Keera walked over and sat on the bed beside her.

Ness shook her head and forced a smile. "It's okay, this is what was always supposed to happen. Everything will go on as if I wasn't here," Ness said.

"But you are here," Keera replied.

"I have to agree, Ness," Sinéad said. "I have always gotten along with my brothers' significant others, but I really don't see myself getting along with Trish. She barely spoke to me when I was young and now that I'm back it's like I'm a leper to her. I don't like it."

"You're back for good?" Ness asked. Sinéad nodded.

"It's a surprise. Don't tell anyone," the nineteen-year-old said. "Sean is stupid, Trish is so obviously in love with Innis."

"You saw it too?" Keera asked.

"Kee, anyone with eyes could see it," Sinéad answered.

"It doesn't really matter, now," Ness replied. "He's made his choice and he's going into this wedding with both eyes open. There's nothing we can do about it."

After a moment, Keera looked down. "Promise me you won't hate me?" she whispered.

"Why would I hate you?" Ness asked.

"I kinda hatched a scheme," Keera confessed.

"What kind of scheme?" Ness was skeptical as she set her tea on the nightstand.

"When I saw the electricity between you and Sean that first day at the dock, I knew I had to do something. I sort of sought out ways of getting you guys together," Keera explained.

"What? Why?" Ness breathed.

"Because none of us like Trish. She runs over Sean and lies to all of us," Keera explained. "She's just a bad person and we all love Sean. He's sweet and loving and doesn't deserve to be miserable."

"Keera," Ness looked down and took a deep breath. "It's not your place. Sean and I must make our own decisions."

"I know. I just wanted you to be happy and I wanted Sean who is like a brother to me, to be with someone I actually like hanging out with," Keera said.

"I can't tell you how much it means to me that you care for me that much," Ness started. "But you can't expect things to change overnight. Sean has been with Trish for years. He's only just met me."

"I've seen the way he looks at you," Keera said.

"We all have," Sinéad piped up.

"Please," Ness closed her eyes against the threatening tears. "Let things be."

Keera sighed and squeezed her friend's hand. "I'll stay with you today, if you'd like."

"I would never ask that of you," Ness said. "Sean is family. I'll be fine. We're back in Kerry. What's the worst that can happen? A stampede of sheep?"

"Hey, those sheep are pretty fierce," Keera said, her sparkling eyes making them all bust out laughing until a knock came at the door.

"Keera? Sinéad?" Emmet's voice called. "Are you ready, loves?"

"*Un*fortunately," Keera answered.

Emmet opened the door and leaned against the frame. He looked rather dashing in his suit.

"Hello, handsome," Ness grinned.

"You lookin' at me, kid?" he winked.

"Who else?" she asked.

Emmet laughed. "You sure you'll be all right here alone, Ness?"

"I'll be fine, Em, thanks," she answered.

"As soon as my part is done, I'll come back," he said.

"You don't have to."

"I will, love. I'm only ushering people to their seats, it's going to be a rather small wedding," he explained. "Innis is the best man and Cabhan is the one groomsman."

She nodded and looked over at Sinéad putting the last piece of hair in place.

"What do you think?" Sinéad asked.

"You look beautiful," Ness answered.

Keera smiled and grasped her hands. "It will all be all right, I just know it," she murmured.

Sinéad gave Ness a hug and left with Emmet. Ness heard the door close behind them. Silence descended. Clutching at her chest where her heart hurt, she gasped, buried her face in a pillow, and screamed. Tears flooded her eyes and there was nothing she could do but give in to the heart-wrenching grief that consumed her.

Chapter

Thirty-Six

Ness tried to catch her breath, the pillow soaked in her tears. She had not cried hard in a very long time. The pain was overwhelming, but she knew when she heard the church bells chime in a matter of minutes, indicating the wedding was about to start, she would lose any control she had managed to gain.

Sitting up took the rest of the sparse energy she had left. Deciding she couldn't stay, she needed to leave before Emmet got back. Standing, she went to the closet and pulled out her duffle bag. Grabbing her clothes, she didn't bother to fold them, just stuffed them into her bag. Pausing when she saw the t-shirt Sean had bought for her at Blarney Castle, she touched it gently and closed her eyes letting two more tears fall. She would have enough memories to haunt her without the souvenirs. As if to taunt her, her lips tingled and ached for Sean's kiss.

Pushing all thoughts aside, she zipped her bag, found her carry on and pulled out the book she had read on the plane. Opening the main cover, she took a pen and wrote an inscription. She set the book on Emmet's pillow for him to find when he returned. Finding a note pad, she wrote a message to Deirdre and Orin and especially Siobhan thanking them for their kindness.

Trying to think of what to leave Keera, the perfect idea came to her. Rushing back to her room, she pulled out the black dress Keera bought for her to wear on the canal barge. Laying it out on the bed, Ness wrote a quick note and set it on the dress with a pin she found in the dresser drawer.

Finally feeling like she had sufficiently thanked everyone, apart from Sean, she quickly went through the house and headed to the front door. Turning the knob, it wouldn't budge. She tried again, still it wouldn't budge. Grabbing the lock in her hand, she tried to turn it, but it wouldn't move.

"Going somewhere?" A voice from behind her made her entire body go cold. Turning, she came face to face with Tyler. "I didn't think so. Daddy's home and I'm very angry with you."

Ness gulped down the bile that rose in her throat. She had nowhere to run.

Chapter

Thirty-Seven

"You're dead," Ness breathed.

"Doesn't look like it. Your aim was a little off," Tyler grinned. "If you want to kill someone... do it right."

She tried to rush past him, but he grabbed her so tightly her shirt ripped at the shoulder.

"Let me go!" she screamed.

"Oh, I *love* it when you beg!" he shouted in triumph. "You've taken me on quite a goose chase. I'm afraid you've been naughty girl."

He picked her up and slammed her against the wall. She cried out when her back hit a picture frame. His mouth and body covered hers, pinning her to the wall. His hands ran down to her chest as he cupped her breasts. She tried to fight him. Biting his lip hard, she spat out the blood. Tyler yelped, released her, and smacked her face. She fell to the ground.

The church bells rang the hour. She could only hope Emmet would be on his way soon. If she could survive the next few minutes, he would help her. She was no match for Tyler. Looking past Tyler, she saw the backdoor. Taking a deep breath, she steeled herself against what he would do to her, but if she could just get outside and scream maybe someone would be able to hear her.

Without another thought, she rose up enough to punch him squarely in the crotch. Tyler cried out and doubled over onto the floor. She didn't wait around to hear his shouts. Racing to the backdoor, she threw it open and ran around to the front of the house screaming for help as she went. Her cheek throbbed and her heart pounded.

Running... Running... Running. She could hear Tyler cursing behind her. Up the hill, *there's the church*, she thought.

Chancing a look back, he was much closer than she realized. He reached out to grab her, but her feet tangled, and she felt herself falling. Tyler grabbed her arm and together they tumbled over a cliff.

Sean stood at the front of the church with Innis at his side. They hadn't spoken since the day before at the dance studio and it was too late to change the programs, tux, and best man. Innis stood silently beside him. Sean still itched to punch him.

The music stopped and the church bells chimed the top of the hour. Emmet nodded at him and slipped out the back apparently heading home to be with Ness. Something Sean wished he could do more and more. The doors to the church closed and the music started up again.

Sean heard Innis's gasp when the doors opened. Looking up, he saw Trish, absolutely stunning, walking down the aisle on her father's arm. She locked eyes with him, and Sean smiled at her, but she did not smile back. Instead, her eyes drifted to Innis and Sean clenched his jaw.

Looking back at his brother, Sean saw a look on his face he had never seen before. Innis was on the verge of tears. Finally, Trish turned back to Sean and set her sights on getting to the front of the church. When she reached the altar, Sean took her hand. The music stopped and as Sean turned to kneel before the priest, Trish pulled back.

"Sean, I need to speak to you," she whispered.

"Now?" he hissed.

"I need to tell you something."

Sean sighed, his eyes scanning the guests. "Can we do this some other time?"

"Sean," she started. "I'm pregnant." Sean's eyes grew wide in shock. Her gaze drifted over to Innis. "You are the father, Innis."

Innis stared at her. His entire body went slack. As if there was no one else around them, he rushed to her, framed her face, and kissed her. Sean's body tingle as rage rushed through his body. His hands clenched and he grabbed Innis' shoulder, forcing him to turn.

Sean's fist collided with Innis' jaw sending him reeling to the floor. A ruckus broke out as Trish screamed and raced to Innis's aid. Cabhan came up behind Sean and held his arms back. A string of insults, some in English, some in Irish flew from Sean's lips.

"Let go of me," he shouted. His eldest brother did not release him.

The guests sitting in the pews, stood shouting trying

to figure out what was going on. Still, Cabhan held Sean firmly as Sean demanded to be released in between issuing a string of obscenities directed at Innis who was still on the floor. Anger radiated from Sean and if Innis stood, Sean wouldn't hold back.

Then, a voice rose above all the others as Emmet burst through the church doors.

"Sean!" Emmet yelled. "She's gone!" Surprise registered on his face as he looked around the room. But not wasting any more time, he clarified. "Ness is gone!"

"What? What do you mean gone?" Sean demanded.

"I mean, I got home just a few minutes ago, like, and found a bicycle lock on the outside front door. I went around back and the door was wide open. She left a note on the counter saying she couldn't stay here any longer. But her bags are still by the door! I don't like it, Sean. Something is wrong."

Shrugging Cabhan off, Sean raced down the aisle and out the doors, Emmet close on his heels.

Orin, Dermott, and their wives tried to calm the crowd as everyone demanded to know what was going on.

"Cabhan, go with them!" Orin called to his first born.

Cabhan nodded and, as he passed Innis still on the ground, offered him a hand up. The disappointment in his eyes made Innis cringe. Brenda rushed to her daughter and held her close.

"It's all right, my dearest," she stroked Trish's hair.

"Oh, mama," Trish cried into her shoulder. "I know I should feel ashamed to have let it go on for so long. And I know I should feel something over losing Sean, but I don't. He should be happy, and we would have never made each other happy. I regret doing this to him, but I am not sorry. He could never make me happy."

"Then who will, my love?" Brenda asked.

"I don't deserve to be," Trish let her tears roll down her cheeks. "Oh god, mama, I am such a terrible person! I was going to trap a good and honest man. How could I have done that?"

"Sweetheart, it's all right," Brenda went on. "You thought he was to be your husband. You never thought you would love another."

"I don't think I ever really loved him," Trish admitted. "I was in love with the idea of being in love. Innis was right. I was founding my marriage on a lie."

Brenda cupped her daughter's jaw and stared into her eyes.

"I'm sorry," Trish finally said.

"Never you mind about all that, your father and I will take care of everything," Brenda said. Dermott touched his daughter's shoulder. Turning, Trish cried into his chest.

"Our main concern is your happiness, love," Dermott said.

"What should I do, daddy? Tell me," she sobbed.

"You have done the right thing in letting him go," Dermott replied. "Be happy for him. Your mother and I will protect you, help you, and your wee one. We love you, darlin', know that."

"I do," she said.

Watching the exchange between Brenda, Dermott, and Trish, Innis locked eyes with Dermott. Nodding once,

Innis let his heart soar when Dermott agreed. Trish pulled away from her father and looked at her parents. Innis took that moment to slide his hand into hers. She looked up at him, her beautiful hazel eyes petrified.

"I love you," he finally said. Gasping, Trish stared at him.

"Do you? Do you really? After everything I did?" she asked.

"Ach, woman, I'll love ya till my dying day," Innis said.

Grasping her to him, he finally could kiss her without worry or fear of exposure. He could claim her before everyone. He could finally have the love he always said he never wanted. He wanted her.

The priest cleared his throat.

"Sorry, Father," Innis apologized as they pulled away from each other.

"I take it then that there will be no wedding today?" the priest asked.

"I'm sorry to have wasted your time, Father," Trish said wiping her tears.

"No," Innis replied. "There *will* be a wedding."

"Innis, look around you," she said.

"There will be a wedding," he repeated looking at Dermott then Brenda.

"Sean will never marry me now," she said. "And I could never do that to him."

"Good," Innis answered. She gasped when he lowered to one knee and took her hands. "Marry *me*, Trisha Riley."

Her tears came faster. "Are you sure?"

"As sure as anything. I love you. I want to make a life with you. I want to have my baby with you. If you'll have me."

"Yes, yes, Innis," she said without any hesitation. "Yes with all my heart, yes I'll have you. I love you too!"

Innis grinned, stood, and kissed her again. Tucking her into his side, he turned to the priest. "Father, will you marry us?" he asked.

"It's about high time, wouldn't you agree?" the priest answered raising an eyebrow. "Would either of you care to say a confession before we start?"

"I would," Innis said turning to Trish. "Trisha Riley, I confess that I love you more than life itself. I confess that you have made me the happiest I've ever been, and I confess to wanting this marriage, this baby, and this family with every fiber of my being. I love you and I will use every day for the rest of our lives to prove it to you. That is my confession."

"Not exactly what I meant, lad, but it'll do," the priest replied.

Chapter

Thirty-Eight

"She couldn't have just disappeared," Sean growled as he thrust his hands through his hair.

"Then, where the hell is she?" Emmet demanded. "I have a sick feeling, Sean. What if something happened while we were gone?"

"If anything happened to her, I swear to god," Sean started.

"I know!" Emmet agreed.

"Sean! Over here!" Cabhan yelled. Sean and Emmet started running. When they saw Cabhan standing at the same cliff Ness had tripped down a week ago, Sean gasped.

"No, dear god no," he shouted. Reaching their eldest brother, "where?" Sean demanded.

Cabhan looked stricken and merely pointed. The

sheer rock face led down to an extremely shallow river. Sean's stomach heaved and his chest felt like it would explode but he forced himself to look.

About twenty feet down, Ness lay on the one rock ledge, surrounded by a pool of blood. Her right arm was flung over the side of a narrow surface, one leg lay straight and the other was bent in a horrible angle with her bone sticking out of her shin through the jeans she wore. Sean's family came up behind him. Keera and Sinéad looked over and shrieked. Without a moment's thought, Sean tore off his tux jacket and tossed it to his father.

"Sean, don't be a fool, that's a twenty-foot drop!" Orin cried.

"It's fine, da'," Sean answered. "I'm not leaving her down there alone."

"We'll call for ropes, wait for those," Cabhan said.

"I'm not waiting a moment longer," Sean replied. "Look at her!" Dermott and Brenda headed their way along with Innis and Trish. "Keep him away from me," Sean growled in a threatening tone.

Brenda saw them looking over the edge and broke into a run. When she reached the cliff, she looked over, and let out a screech. Cabhan held her so she would fall.

"Save her! Please save my baby!" Brenda cried.

"What?" Sean breathed. Everyone stared.

"Mama?" Trish asked.

"Sean, please save my daughter!" she cried. Dermott took his wife from Cabhan and held her tightly to him.

"All will be explained," Dermott promised. "Please, Sean."

Sean nodded.

"What can I do?" Innis stepped forward.

"Stay the hell away from my woman," Sean growled. Innis took a step back and raised his hands in surrender.

Looking back at Emmet, who nodded, they latched arms and Emmet slowly lowered him down the slope. Once Sean was far enough to slide the rest of the way, Emmet released his arm. After a couple of heart-stopping moments, Sean finally reached the ledge where Ness lay.

"Ness, Nessa," he frantically checked her pulse, sick with worry he was too late. Relief coursed through him as he felt a beat. "She's alive!" He called.

The shriek from Brenda and the other women echoed across the valley.

"Don't move her!" Cabhan called, his mobile at his ear. "The best paramedics in the county are on their way. Tell me what you're seeing."

Sean nodded and went back to examine her. She was unconscious so he checked her head. A knot the size of an egg was forming at the base of her skull. Looking over at her arm, he saw the redness on her shoulder as her arm hung over the side, the ball clearly out of her socket.

"Her left shoulder is dislocated," Sean called up. "And she has a lump the size of a goose egg on the back of her head."

"Try not to let her move if she wakes up," Cabhan said. "See if you can move her arm to her chest but don't move her shoulder."

Sean reached over and grasped her wrist. Gently pulling her arm to her chest, distress registered on her face and she groaned.

"Ness?" he called softly. "Ness, can you hear me, love?"

"Sean," she moaned.

"I'm here," he said. "Can you open your eyes, love?"

Slowly her eyelids fluttered and opened a crack. Her glazed and unfocused gaze locked with his, she screamed and tried to fight him, yelling over and over again that he couldn't have her. Sean grabbed her hand gently and did the only thing he knew would distract her. Leaning down, he kissed her. She froze, then went limp and kissed him back. When he finally pulled away, her eyes focused on him.

"Sean?" she whispered, stroking his jaw with her finger.

"Yes, love, I'm here," he said.

Commotion behind him made him turn. Emmet slid down the ledge to them.

"How is she?" Emmet asked, concern lining his face.

"She woke," Sean replied.

"Emmet?" Ness asked softly.

"Aye, girl, I'm here," Emmet answered.

"Where's Tyler?" Ness asked.

Both brothers looked at each other, their worst fears coming true. They had left her alone and Tyler had nearly killed her.

"What happened, love?" Sean asked.

"I... he chased me, and we fell, I think," she replied.

Emmet gazed over the ledge and flinched.

"He won't be botherin' you anymore, Ness," Emmet said. Sean looked at his brother who motioned his head. Tyler had missed the ledge and fell the rest of the way down.

"Sean," Ness said softly.

"Yes?" he asked.

"My leg hurts."

"Yeah, it's broken, darlin'."

She nodded almost as if she couldn't register what was going on.

"You scared the bejesus out of me, love," Sean said.

"He's not the only one," Emmet concurred.

"My arm hurts too," she said softly.

"Your shoulder is dislocated," Sean explained.

"Okay," she sighed and closed her eyes.

"Cabhan said to keep her alert," Emmet said.

Sean nodded and leaned down to kiss her again. Her eyes flew open when he pressed his lips to hers. With her good hand she shoved him away.

"Sean," she breathed. "You are a married man."

"No, love, I'm not," he answered. "I didn't marry Trish. I couldn't. I love you."

Ness looked at him. "That's not fair," she said.

Sean blinked. "Ehm, what's not fair, love?"

"I'm not going to remember this," she said. "I won't remember you telling me you love me."

"Well, I'll make a deal wit ya," Sean started. "Get better and I'll be tellin' you every day till you get sick of hearing it."

"I'll never get sick of hearing it," she replied.

He grinned and kissed her again.

"Ugh, I hate happily-ever-afters. They're so tacky," Emmet groaned.

Ness giggled and looked at him. "You'll love it when it happens to you," she said. "I'll convert you to hot and steamy romances yet."

"I saw your gift to me," Emmet replied. "That's when I knew something was wrong. Never do that to me again."

"Leave you a romance novel?" She asked.

"Leave me without a proper goodbye," Emmet choked.

"I love you, Emmet," she said.

"I love ya too, darlin'," he replied. "And if you're ever tinkin' about scaring the bejesus out of me again... don't."

Ness smiled. Looking up at Sean she stroked his face. "Sean?" she whispered.

"Aye, love?" he asked.

"Now that you're not married... don't think for one moment you're going to push me away," she said.

"Don't worry, darlin'," he said. "That'll never happen."

Chapter

Thirty-Nine

Blinding lights and an annoying beeping greeted Ness as she slowly opened her eyes. Blinking hard, she tried to open her eyes wider but a dull throb in her right shoulder and leg drew her attention.

She groaned and suddenly the light above her was blotted out as a familiar face hovered over her.

"Ness?" Sean's face was drawn, dark circles rimmed his eyes, and at least three days' worth of beard growth covered his jaw.

She paused a moment to take him in, the beard made him look even sexier. Weakly, she raised her left arm since her right wouldn't budge. Smiling when he leaned into her touch and trapped her hand against his face with his shoulder, she sighed, "hi."

"Hello," he breathed.

"What happened?"

"I was hoping you would tell me," he said. "You didn't make much sense at the cliff. But first let me get you a nurse," he reached around her and pressed the nurse call button. Ness reveled in the feeling of him being so close. Before he pulled back, he dropped a kiss on her forehead. She moaned a happy sound and he chuckled. "Do you remember anything?" he asked.

"I remember pain and I get flashes of you but nothing else," she answered.

"You scared the life out of me," he said.

She looked down. "How's your wife?"

"Happily married to the father of her child," he said. Ness looked up at him confused. "She and Innis are pregnant," he spat. "They married, not me."

"You're not married?"

"No, love," he answered. "The woman I love is here before me."

She choked back a happy sob as the nurse walked in.

"Good morning, Nessa," she smiled. "I am Nurse Maggie. Do you know where you are?"

"Hospital," she answered simply.

"That's right," she replied. "We had you air lifted to Dublin. Can you tell me your name?"

"Nessa Rylie Alexander," she said.

"Good and what's your birthday?" the nurse asked.

"August seventh."

"And do you know this man?" the nurse asked gesturing to Sean. Ness nodded. "Who is he?" she prodded gently.

"Sean O'Quinn, the love of my life," she said. Sean grinned.

"Good then," the nurse beamed. "I'll fetch the doctor."

"Can I get up?"

"You can sit up yes, but you'll have to wait until the doctor okay's you to get out of bed. You had a compound fracture in your right leg."

Ness flinched but nodded. Once the nurse had left the room, Sean took her hand and looked away.

"Hey, what's wrong, baby?" she asked.

He looked over at her and smiled slightly. "Say it again."

"What?" she asked.

"What you called me."

She grinned. "Baby."

"I like that," he replied. After a moment, he continued softly. "You scared me, love."

"I'm sorry," she answered.

"When Emmet ran into the church to tell me you left, my world had blackened with Trish's revelation but my whole life shattered around me when I realized what he was saying. You had left me, and I hadn't been able to say I loved you. I thought we could go on the way we were, but I realized I had been the worst of eejits. Paradise was looking me in the eyes, and I ignored it for some stupid macho measuring contest with my brother. I don't love Trish. I thought I did, but I don't. Not like I love you. I stole your heart and gave you mine, but I wasn't man enough to take a chance to risk a pseudo happiness for a chance at paradise. Can you forgive me?"

Ness stared into his toffee colored eyes and smiled. Holding his hand, she yanked him down to her. He hovered over her; his lips quirked in a smirk.

"Has anyone ever told you, you talk too much?" she whispered.

"Yes," he replied. "But it is so sexy coming from you."

"Well, then, Mr. O'Quinn, shut up and kiss me," she said.

"Why, Ms. Alexander, it would be my pleasure," he replied lowering his lips to hers.

The stolen kisses throughout the past few days were wonderful, but without the fear of being caught, they were able to kiss each other like Ness had never thought possible. Everything vanished around them. Holding on to each other as their lips danced in the most provocative way, they both never wanted it to end. It wasn't until Sean felt a tap on his shoulder that he finally pulled away.

Looking back, Emmet stood behind him with the doctor, both had amused grins on their faces.

"I assume the young lady is feeling better then?" the doctor asked.

"Much better," Ness giggled. "Far better if you two would leave and let him continue."

"Aye, I like that option," Sean winked back at her.

Emmet and the doctor chuckled. "So, I guess this means I've lost me chance wit ye, love?" Emmet teased.

"I like to keep my options open," she winked.

"Oh really?" Sean laughed. "Are ya sure about that, love? Don't be thinkin' this eejit is better than me?"

Ness laughed then groaned reaching for her shoulder. The doctor stepped forward and started examining the joint. Emmet pulled Sean aside. They watched the doctor work and once he had finished, asked him if she was all right.

"Don't overdo it. Once you start feeling tired, rest, until then, sit up and have something to eat," the doctor encouraged.

Sean and Emmet sat on the sides of the bed once they were alone.

"Have you looked at yourselves in the mirror?" Ness asked them. They both looked at her confused. "How did one family have such hot guys as sons?"

"They take after their da'," a voice by the door drew their attention.

Ness smiled when she saw Orin, Deirdre, Sinéad, Keera, and Siobhan standing there.

"Hey, guys," Ness said.

"The doctor said you were awake, love," Orin went on. "We wanted to come and see ya. Make sure me boys were behaving themselves."

"Well, *Emmet* has been a complete gentleman," Ness giggled.

"*That* I'll never believe," Sinéad replied following Keera and hugging her.

"Sean… well, he's been a bit of a rogue and I love it," she teased him.

"Good, then they've done me proud," Orin smiled.

"We are so very glad you're awake," Deirdre replied. "The note you left was so moving, my dear. But we are very grateful you haven't left us."

Ness thanked her as she gave her hand a squeeze. "I'm glad I didn't leave either."

"Besides, somebody has to keep my brothers in line," Sinéad smiled. "You know Sean and Emmet are the worst ones."

"Oh, I would agree," Ness answered. "The worst ones for causing a girl to fall helplessly in love." Then she looked around, feeling a little guilty she didn't include all the brothers. "Where's Cabhan?" she asked.

"Rae was having some pains so he stayed with her, but he's been grilling the doctors on your care," Deirdre said.

"Is she okay?" Ness asked concerned.

"Nothing but nerves. She was very worried for you," Deirdre explained.

"I'm sorry," Ness said. "I hope the baby is okay."

"She told me to tell you everything is all right and she wants to see you when you're awake," Deirdre answered.

"I'd like that."

A small noise came from behind them and they all turned to see Brenda Riley standing in the doorway. Ness looked at Trish's mother, confused.

"May I have a moment?" Brenda asked. Ness gripped Sean's hand.

"It's all right. I'll stay with you," he offered.

"Everything is all right, dear," Deirdre assured. "We'll leave you both." Sending Brenda an affectionate look, she ushered everyone out of the room.

Once they were alone, Brenda wrung her hands and paced in front of the door. Ness watched her for a long moment then looked over at Sean. He smiled and squeezed her hand.

"I – ehm, hardly know where to begin," Brenda started. "I suppose..." she broke off and took a deep breath. "Ness," she finally turned to her. "Did you know that you were adopted?"

Chapter

Forty

Ness's brows drew together. "How do you know?" she asked. Sean gently stroked her arm. "Did you tell her?" she asked him. Sean shook his head.

"Ness, when I was a much younger woman, I was in love with Dermott's elder brother, Liam Riley. He was a good bit older than me, seven years in fact. But I loved him so incredibly fiercely. He was everything to me..."

Ness was staring at her, not saying a word.

"After dating for five years, we broke up amicably," Brenda went on. "And after a little while, Dermott expressed his interest in me. With Liam's blessing, we began dating. After a time, Dermott proposed. We were so happy together and Liam claimed he was happy for us but soon the wedding planning took our attention and we started seeing Liam less and less.

"Eventually Dermott asked his brother to be his best man, but Liam refused, saying he could not come to the wedding at all, let alone stand beside him. That surprised us because we thought Liam was all right with everything. Without another word, he left, and we did not see him again for many years. Dermott and I were so unbelievably happy together and we moved past it all. When Trisha came along, our life was complete.

"One day..." she choked. "I was in Belfast visiting my aunt while Dermott was away for six months in England for work. I saw Liam by accident for the first time in five years. We both seemed excited to see each other and acted like no time had passed. He asked me to join him for a pint at the local. We talked for hours and drank far too much," she swallowed hard. "We... ehm... went to the hotel and well... ya have to understand, he was the love of my life and as much as I love Dermott, Liam... there was a supernatural cosmic pull to each other.

"When I awoke the next morning, he was gone. He had left me a note on the pillow telling me he would always love me but he couldn't be with me, betray his brother again or allow any close connection because of what he did for a living. I did not realize he was involved with the IRA. And at that time, it was very dangerous.

"I never told Dermott about my one night with Liam," she wiped her tears. "And it was only a week later we got the news Liam was killed in an IRA retaliation bombing in Northern Ireland. I was devastated and only had myself to console since I could not tell my husband of my... indiscretion.

"Two months after he died, I wasn't feeling well and went to our local doctor. He told me I was... pregnant. I knew immediately it was Liam's child since Dermott had been gone for four months.

"I was devastated but incredibly happy at the same time. I knew I could not lie to Dermott and pass off his brother's child as his own, what if the baby had her father's piercing green eyes? So, I did the hardest thing I've ever done. I called Dermott in London and told him I was accepted for a semester to teach in America. I left without telling him I was pregnant.

"I had the baby in Chicago, a beautiful baby girl and she did have her father's eyes. I held her once and named her Rylie, giving her his last name as a middle name," her voice cracked with tears. Her first name was my mother's, Vanessa.

"She was so beautiful, and I loved her so much. I did not want to give her up, but I was scared. I was told she was placed with a wonderful couple and I closed the adoption. When I went back to Ireland, I was able to act as if nothing happened but inside, I was breaking. I prayed for her every night and I never thought I'd see my baby again... especially not here in Ireland." Brenda broke off and stared into Ness's piercing green eyes.

"Are you..." Ness cleared her throat. "Are you my mother?"

Brenda nodded. "Vanessa Rylie Alexander, I am your mother. And I can only hope you forgive me for everything I've done and couldn't do. I recognized you the moment I saw you. You look so much like me at your age but with Liam's eyes."

Ness stared at her for a long moment. "I always wanted to meet my birth parents. I always knew I was adopted. The Alexanders were wonderful people but I was always missing something. My dad, my adopted dad," she clarified. "Always told me that my parents were from Ireland but I didn't know if I would ever meet them."

"I can only hope you can understand and can forgive me. I wanted you so much but I couldn't keep you."

"I do understand," Ness said. "Who knows how any of us would have reacted in the same predicament? I am glad to meet you. Forgive me if this isn't the joyful reunion we wanted."

"Sweetheart, no, you're hurt. I just couldn't wait any longer to tell you."

"I had a good life," she said. "Up until sixteen I loved everything about my life. Thank you for giving me life. I'm sure this will all come crashing down on me soon but... can I call you... mama?"

Brenda let out a sob. "You can call me anything you want, darling."

Ness lifted her hand and Brenda rushed to her, taking her offering. Brenda sat on the bed and wrapped Ness in a warm embrace. She felt like home. Something about Brenda gave Ness a sort of peace she never understood and she let the tears fall.

After a long moment, Ness pulled back to see Brenda crying happy tears too. "I wish I could have met my father."

Brenda slipped some of Ness's hair behind her ear. "He would have loved you," she whispered. "He always wanted a child and a daughter most of all. He wanted to spoil you. He said, he would be her white knight and only the best could woo her away from him."

Ness laughed and chanced to look at Sean as he wiped a tear from his eye.

"I always thought my da' was a king in some far-off land and he would come find me one day and call me his princess. I would give my heart to the king's champion and he would love me, and we would live happily ever after. Then when my dad died, and my mom married Tyler, all my innocent fantasies wound up disappearing. All I wanted was to get away." Ness smiled sadly. "I wish I could have known him."

"Would knowing your uncle count, love?" Dermott's voice, thick with emotion, came from the doorway. Ness and Brenda looked over at him. "You may be me brother's daughter, but I would be honored if you would look upon me as an adopted father."

Ness nodded and reached for him. Dermott embraced and kiss them both.

"You're me wife's daughter, me wee darlin'," he went on. "I knew when I saw ya at the pub, so like your mother ye are," Dermott wiped tears from his eyes. "With me brother's green eyes I never thought I'd see again. I loved Liam. It hurt me deeply when we parted under those circumstances, but we can tell ye all about your father, love. He was a great man."

Ness couldn't stop her tears. But soon Trish appeared in the doorway.

"I guess this means we're sisters," Trish said softly. "And cousins."

"And we're in love with two brothers," Ness laughed.

"I guess we're gonna have to get used to each other," she smiled.

"Sisters?" Ness offered.

"Sisters," Trish confirmed. They hugged each other tightly.

"Sean told me you and Innis are married," Ness said.

Trish nodded smiling. "I'm lucky he still wanted me," Trish replied. Sean barely suppressed his snort.

"Congratulations to you both and for the baby," Ness said.

Trish put a hand to her still flat stomach. "It's hard to

believe but Innis isn't letting me do anything. He's pampering me." Both women giggled but Ness saw Sean roll his eyes.

"We should let her rest," Sean said.

"Oh, of course," Brenda replied standing from the hospital bed.

"Ach, he just wants her for himself," Dermott laughed.

"And rightfully so," Brenda replied. "Do you not remember how you were when we were their age?" Brenda winked at her husband.

With a low growl and a flash of desire in his eyes, Dermott pulled his wife into him. "At their age?" he asked. "Woman, I *still* want you to myself."

Brenda laughed flirtatiously and tenderly slapped her husband's chest. "Ya rogue ya," she winked.

Trish looked back at Ness. "Thank god there's someone else to suffer with me through their *moments*."

Ness laughed but waved goodbye to the three of them. Once they were finally alone, Sean sat back down on the bed and took her hand.

"Are you all right?" he asked wiping her tears off her cheeks.

"I never thought I would know who I really am," she stated. "I never thought I would find true love, my real mother, and my identity when Keera asked me to come with her."

Sean cupped her face. "I expected to be in the Bahamas with a wife I never really loved, living a life I never really wanted. I never expected to be in the hospital with a woman I can honestly say is the love of my life, anxiously waiting for the future," Sean said giving her a kiss.

"Please don't be angry with Trish and Innis," she said. "I know they lied to you and betrayed you but for my sake, please. Take it from someone who never had a family. They are a blessing."

"Love," he sighed. "I'm gonna need more than three days to get over this."

"It's been three days?" She asked. He nodded. "Just promise me you'll try."

"For you, my love, I would do anything," he sighed. "But I cannot go back to exactly the way it was. Innis was my best friend and my brother. He betrayed me and then lied about it. I will be civil, even friendly, but it will take more than just a few days, if ever, for me to fully trust him again."

"I respect that," she said.

"Now, you need your rest," he replied softly standing and shaking out a blanket.

"I can't sleep," she sighed. "Not with the excitement of everything that's happened."

"You need to try," he replied helping her lie down. "How are you feeling?"

"I'm okay. My shoulder is throbbing, and my leg is hurting but okay."

"Oh, baby," he stroked her face gently. "When I saw you on the ledge," he broke off and shook his head. "I thought my heart would stop when I saw your legbone sticking out."

"Really?" She shuttered.

"I've never been so scared," he admitted. "Ness, I love you so much."

She reached up and pulled him down to her. She kissed him gently and then whispered against his lips. "I love you too."

He kissed her lightly again and gently rubbed his nose against hers. She giggled at his touch.

"You need your rest," he replied. "What kind of boyfriend would I be if I prevented you from getting your proper sleep?"

"The best," she teased.

"Now, Ness," he pretended to scold her. "Love, you need to rest to heal. You've had a bit of a rough go of it. Rest, that way you will heal quicker." She laughed as he winked and tucked the blankets around her.

Then he turned to leave. "Hey," she grasped his hand. "Don't leave me."

"Ha! I haven't left your side for three days. Now that you're awake, you will get sick of seeing me," he said.

"I'll never be sick of seeing you. Or hearing you say you love me."

"Ya crazy," he chortled. "So you *do* remember."

She bit her lower lip to prevent her grin. "It might be one of the flashes from the mountain ledge I still recall."

Sean threw his head back and laughed. Pulling a chair up to the side of the bed, he kept her hand in his and sat. He grabbed a remote and aimed it at the television, turning it on.

"Sean?" she said after a moment. He looked over at her.

"Yes?"

"I love you."

"I will never get tired of hearing that either," he said. Then looking toward the door and back at her, he pulled off his shoes and slipped under the sheets. She snuggled into him.

"I was hoping you would do this," she mumbled into his chest. She felt him chuckle silently and kiss her head then turn back to the television. The light changed subtly as he flicked through the channels. "Sean?"

"Aye, baby?" he asked.

"When are we going out on our first date?" she questioned.

"Soon," he promised with a kiss on her head. "Very soon."

With that, she fell into a deep sleep, her Irishmen, her O'Quinn, her love pressed to her side and a bright happy future ahead of her.

Epilogue

Six Months Later

Ness heard the doorbell and hurried to the door. Squealing with delight as Trish waddled in, the sisters embraced.

"Oh, this heat!" Trish said dramatically wiping pretend sweat from her forehead. "I was lucky to get away. Innis keeps worrying. He thinks his daughter will be early and wants us to get back to Dublin."

"I bet, but I'm so glad you're here!" Ness said closing the door behind her.

"Oh, so am I," Trish said. "Is your husband as controlling as mine?"

Ness giggled. "Not yet, but maybe in six months when I look like you... he just might be."

"What?" Trish squealed. "Are you pregnant?"

"I just found out today," Ness grinned.

"Oh, darlin'!" Trish gushed. "That didn't take him long, did it?" Trish wiggled her eyebrows suggestively.

"Well, we have been married for four months," Ness giggled. "And... um... well, Sean is rather... let's just say I knew it wouldn't take us too long, if you know what I mean."

Both women laughed. "Oh love, I am so thrilled for you!" Trish said. "We have to go baby clothes shopping!"

"Oh, I would love that," Ness replied.

"When are you going to tell him?"

"Tonight. He's teaching right now."

"How's he liking it?"

"Oh, he loves it!" Ness smiled. "He says the boys are fast learners and he always has this look of wanting one of our own. I can't wait to tell him."

"So, what are your ideas? How are you going to tell him?" Trish sat back with a cup of tea in her hand.

Sean noticed he always had a smile on his lips for the past six months. Ness had healed quickly, and they were married four months after they found her on the cliff ledge. Tyler's body had been discovered with nearly every bone broken and his head bashed in from the fall. Emmet and Cabhan took care of the Garda and their endless questions. Ness was in the hospital for a couple of weeks and in physical therapy for over a month. Sean had stayed by her side throughout everything and they were soon engaged. His friends called him daft but all he knew was, he was the happiest he had ever been.

As he pulled his new car into the driveway, he remembered how Emmet had finally convinced him to sell

Ole Bess and get a new one, one perfect for a married man, eager for a family but still professional enough for the future Headmaster of Kerry County schools.

Parking the car and grabbing his briefcase containing his pupils' tests, he strolled up to the front door, suddenly eager to see his wife.

"Nessa?" he called as he walked in. Slipping out of his shoes, he smelled something delicious wafting through the kitchen. "Ness? Where are you, love?"

"Stay there for a minute, baby!" he smiled when he heard her.

"I'm staying," he teased.

"Promise?"

"Yeah, yeah," he grinned.

"Good. Close your eyes."

Sighing, he obliged.

"Are they closed?" She asked.

"Of course," he called back. "But, love, is this any way to greet your husband after he's had a long day's work?" he teased.

"Oh, trust me," he loved that silky sensual tone she had. "It's the *perfect* way."

A smirk crossed his lips as he felt her standing in front of him.

"Open your eyes, husband," she whispered.

Sean didn't hesitate. Ness was holding a small cake, half with blue icing and half with pink icing. Each side had a single corresponding colored lit candle. He smiled.

"What are you on about?" he wondered, then he read

the words she had written in icing.

Boy or Girl

His eyes shot up to hers, she grinned. "Well? Which one do you want it to be?" she asked innocently.

He couldn't speak. He stared at her. "You're – we're pre – pregnant?" he stuttered.

Her grin widened as she nodded. "Uh huh."

He felt the giggles start up his throat and erupt from his mouth, his smile was so wide his cheeks hurt. Blowing out the candles, he set the cake aside, picked her up and twirled her around, both laughing with joy. Finally, he set her down slowly bracing her body against his.

"I love you," he swore.

"I love you too, my Irishman," she said running her fingers through his hair.

He kissed her like he had never kissed her before. She was no longer just his wife, his lover, she was the mother of his child. For the millionth time in the past six months, he thanked his brother. Had Innis not fought for what he wanted, Sean would never have had that moment, his love, and his woman.

Before they were too far gone to speak, Ness pulled back. "But you still haven't answered the question. Which do you want? A boy or a girl?"

Sean thought a moment. "A girl with red hair and the deepest green eyes," he decided.

"Are you sure?" she asked with a teasing lilt. "If she's too beautiful you'll have to fight off all the men chasing after her."

"Ooh, you are absolutely right. But you know..." he

smirked. "No red-haired lass is safe here, under the Irish sky... and I mean *no* lass," he winked. She giggled as he picked her up, carried her to their room, shut the door behind him, and showed her how much he loved her.

an deireadh

Acknowledgements

Acknowledgements are the hardest part of an author's day. We never want to leave anyone out but it's inevitable. So ,to start with:

My family. Mama, Dad, and Cameron. You have always been there for me in everything I've done. Thank you for encouraging me to try my hand at something different and challenging me to stretch myself in writing. You are amazing and I love you!

To Danny, our amazing tour guide from our tour to Scotland and Ireland. You were so wonderful to answer all of my questions about customs and everyday life in Ireland!

Lastly, to my ancestors. Ireland is home to so many but when I stepped onto the shores of that magical island, I felt you all welcoming me home. Sláinte!

Read on for a sneak peek at Emmet's story *Across the Irish Sea* now available!

Please keep an eye out on my website for more new releases! www.mkatherineclark.net

love among the shamrocks collection

Book Two

ACROSS THE IRISH SEA

M. KATHERINE CLARK

CHAPTER

ONE

Emmet O'Quinn adjusted his tie and leaned back in his desk chair. Raising his arms, he clasped his hands to the top of his head. The annoying dealership music gnawed on his ears and didn't help his headache. As owner, he intended to do something about it. There's only so many times he could endure *Galway Girl* or *Yellow Brick Road*. The eclectic radio station was new to the area and asked him to be a sponsor to drum up more publicity. As the only dealership and mechanics in ten miles, he agreed. But at that moment, he would rather claw his ears than hear another Irish Jig.

Closing his eyes for a moment to give at least one sensory overload a reprieve, he heard his friend and top salesman come into the office.

"Ya a little soft today, Em?" Paddy asked.

"Nah," Emmet replied. He hadn't finished his one pint last night at the local, so he was far from hung over. "Just a headache, no alcohol involved." No alcohol, but god knew he needed some when he read the letter burning a hole in his cupboard. Even after a week, he still couldn't believe it.

"Hmm, have ye taken anything for it?"

"No," Emmet sighing and opened his eyes, taking his coffee mug. "And since when have you become such a woman? It'll pass soon," he took a gulp of his espresso. Offering a single serve coffee machine out in the waiting area for everyone to use, Emmet kept his espresso maker in his office in case he, Paddy or any other salesman might need a stronger cup than the in bulk Breakfast Blend.

"Want me to take the next ones?" Paddy asked, looking out his window. "A pretty little thing." Emmet raised his head to squint out into the late afternoon sun. "Who's that with her? I can't see from here."

As soon as Emmet's eyes locked on the two women his friend had mentioned, he wished the nineteen eighties linoleum floor would open and drag him down. His ex-fiancée, who was now very much married to his former best friend and five months pregnant with their fourth child, was walking up the drive.

"Oh Jaysus," Emmet breathed. "Of course, why doesn't that surprise me?"

He hadn't seen her for a year. Not since his now sister-in-law, Ness arrived from America and they had gone to Blarney Castle.

"I'd be happy to take this one," Paddy said, eyeing the girl walking beside Chloe.

"I've got it," Emmet replied. Being owner, Emmet could have passed them to someone else, but he didn't like how Paddy was eyeing the woman beside Chloe. "Work is no place to find your next hookup, Paddy." Pulling on his suit jacket, he ran a hand through his auburn hair and went out to greet the two women.

"Chloe," Emmet called, across the parking lot. She looked up and forced a smile.

"Emmet," she greeted when they met halfway. She looked beautiful. Five months pregnant and she glowed. They didn't touch, neither of them offering a hand to each other.

"What brings you out?" He asked.

"My sister, Mara just got back from England and she needs a car to get around. She has a job in Bantry and will be commuting until she's set up." Chloe was saying indicating the younger woman beside her.

The dark-haired woman Paddy had talked about earlier, looked over at him and Emmet's eyes widened.

"Mara?" he asked surprised. "Christ, woman, look at you! You've grown up. You look amazing."

"You don't look too bad yourself, Emmet O'Quinn," she said, her accent subtly Irish.

"How have you been?"

"Good," she answered. "Been in England for a while. Wanted to come back to Ireland when I got the news of Tom's and Chloe's fourth."

"Jaysus," he breathed. "I haven't seen you in, what... at least thirteen years."

"More like fifteen, I think," she said. "I went to Belgium when I was thirteen remember?"

"Saints, I do, girl," he replied. "I remember when you were a child." He couldn't help his eyes trailing over her, taking in all the changes fifteen years had caused. She was beautiful and clearly no longer a child. "You look amazing," he breathed.

Chloe cleared her throat and Emmet felt the weight of her stare. Looking down uncomfortably, he continued. "So, what brings ya to my doorstep?"

"Mara needs a car," Chloe reminded him. "And this is the only dealer near us."

"Right," he replied. "Well, you've come to the right place. What are you looking for?"

"Low emissions, one litre, compact. I'll be staying with Chloe until I can find a place in Bantry," Mara answered.

"You know, a friend of mine down that way is looking to rent the flat over his garage. It's nice. I stayed there for a few months. I think it's only about three hundred euro," he said.

"That sounds pretty perfect actually," she replied.

"I'll give you his number and give him a call, letting him know to expect you," he answered.

"Thanks," she said. "Also, I should say, I need it to be in great nick as I'm not a car mechanic and I don't think I would be comfortable with anything less."

"Ah, I see," Emmet smiled.

"I can't even change a flat," she admitted.

"That's something every girl should know how to do," he said. "I can teach ya."

"I'd like that."

"Tom will be able to teach her, Emmet," Chloe answered.

"Right, of course, sorry," Emmet nodded. "One last question," Emmet turned to Mara again. "Two birds fall out of their nest, one flies, one falls, what kind are they?" She hesitated. "First thing that pops in your mind."

"Robins," she answered. His brows rose. "I know. Stupid."

"Nothing is stupid, just intriguing," he answered. "Follow me."

"Emmet," Chloe called. He turned to her. "I'm sorry. I'm more tired recently. Is there a place I can sit and wait for you?"

"Of course, yeah," he said and waved towards the office. "There's plenty of seats inside. Paddy will help ya."

"Thanks. You good?" she asked her sister. Mara nodded and Chloe headed into the building without another look at Emmet.

He waited for the pang of guilt and perhaps a little jealousy, but it never came. He had loved Chloe, but life put them on separate paths and for once he was glad for her. Tom was a great man. Even if they didn't speak any more, Emmet would always regard him as the best friend he could ever have. Shaking out of his thoughts and turning his attention to the possible sale, he looked back at Mara and they walked together.

"If you don't mind me asking, Emmet," Mara started. "What happened between you and Chloe? You guys were together for nearly five years. Everyone thought you'd get married one day."

"I was an eejit," he answered. "She was too good for me, so I let her go."

"That seems like a very selfless thing to do," Mara said.

"No, it was selfish," he replied. "When we met, I was a kid of sixteen, then my mom died, and I hit a bit of a rough patch in my life. I fell into the wrong crowd and did things I am not proud of. Once that was over, I told Chloe something I regret, and we decided to go our separate ways."

"I'm sorry," Mara said. "It's none of my business. Just one day you were there and the next you were gone, and Chloe was..."

"I know," he breathed. "I would say I'm sorry, but I'm not, because she's with a man who loves her the way she should be loved. Tell me something..." she nodded, and he continued. "Is she happy?"

"Yes," Mara replied. "I won't lie, it was a rough year after you and she broke up and Tom entered the picture. But I know he loves her fiercely and she him. I was angry with you for a long time but then I... don't take this the wrong way... I pitied you. You were always so kind to me and never made me feel like the unwanted baby sister. Chloe had Tom to help her but what about you? You didn't have anyone."

"I didn't need anyone," he lied. "And you were never unwanted. I always enjoyed talking and being around you, even if you were a scrawny little kid," he grinned.

She pretended indignation, slapping him playfully on the arm. "Oh please, at least I grew out of that phase."

"Aye, you did," Emmet stated, his voice low and heavy. "Sorry," he shook his head. "I didn't mean it like that."

"Then how did you mean it?" she questioned, and the timbre of her voice raked up his spine. He scratched the back of his neck and cleared his throat.

"Ehm, enough about me," he said, and she saw a very visible emotional wall go up around him, hiding his true feelings. He stopped in front of the cutest car she'd ever seen. She even like the red color. He crossed his arms over his broad chest and leaned against it. "What do you think?"

"Oh my god!" she exclaimed. "It's adorable!"

"Wanna take it for a drive?" he asked. She nodded emphatically. "I'll go get the keys." Pushing off the car, he headed into the building.

Chapter Two

*D*amn, Emmet thought as he walked into the building to get the keys. Mara was his ex's baby sister and a good eight years younger than him. He repeated those facts again and again, but he couldn't cool his body's response to her. Taking a deep breath, he grabbed the keys out of the wall case. Luckily, he remembered the right ones. Never had he felt such an immediate attraction. True, he had known her for years when they were both kids but that was long ago. She was his ex-fiancée's sister. He was sure somewhere there was a rule written down in stone saying not to angle with that.

Not only could he not afford to be seen with anyone at the moment, he couldn't entertain even for a second, the idea of stepping out with her. Shaking his head to clear it, nothing worked, and he was highly tempted to ask Paddy to help her with the test drive. But even that thought caused a jealous streak he never had before, to race through him so fast he shivered. Any other time he would be interested to explore the feelings stirring inside him, but he was neither free to do so nor would he allow himself to hurt another McGrath woman.

Still consumed by his thoughts as he walked back out to the parking lot, he was surprised to see Mara looking angrily at her phone. She punched a message and hit send. Putting it into her purse, she looked up at him and immediately, seeing a sort of angry fear behind her brown eyes, he rushed to her.

"Everything all right?"

"Great," she answered quickly.

Normally not one to pry but after the adventures with Ness, his sister-in-law, almost a year ago, he didn't like it when a woman had that look. It usually meant they were hiding something or from someone and in over their head.

"Mara," he challenged.

She must have sensed the change because her shoulders deflated, and she finally spoke. "My ex, he won't give up."

"He sounds like an arse," Emmet replied.

"You don't know the half of it," she nonchalantly touched her cheek and Emmet froze. He tried to push away the thought of her touching a place the bastard had bruised often. Still not in a position to do more than distract her, he held out the keys.

"Well," he said tightly. "How about a test drive, then?"

"Sounds good," she smiled.

He tossed her the keys but she shielded her face and the keys fell to the ground.

"I'm sorry. Are you all right?"

"I'm fine, sorry." Reaching down, she picked up the key and without another word, slid in the driver's side.

Explaining some of the features of the car, Emmet watched her through the corner of his eye. Even though she seemed interested in everything he was explaining, he could tell she was still shaken by the text she had received and possibly, him throwing the keys to her. He decided to put the salesman on hold and leaned back in his seat.

"Pull off up here," he said gently.

She looked over at him but agreed. He guided her to the entrance of a parking lot and into one of the spots. Emmet got out and walked around to her side. Opening her door, he offered his hand to help her out. They walked a little way until they came to the top of a small rise.

"Oh my," she sighed. "Emmet, this is beautiful."

"One of my favorite views," he said thinking of how many views he deemed were his favorite. He had shared at least three with Ness over a year ago.

"It's so... secluded," she said, then suddenly looked wary. "Why did you bring me here, alone?"

"I thought you might like it," he shrugged, hating the images flicking through his mind as to why she was so scared.

"Is anyone around?" she wrapped her arms around herself and took a few steps away from him.

"There's a lot of people around," he answered.

She visibly relaxed when he pointed out a couple old fishermen and a father and son bringing in their early afternoon catch.

Seeing the natural beauty of County Kerry, he watched as she relaxed. That is, until her phone vibrated in her handbag. She tried to ignore them but after the twelfth one, Emmet look over at her.

"Sounds important," he said.

"He's not," she stated. "He's just a bastard who needs to learn his favorite toy fights back and if he ever lays another hand on me."

"Did he hit you?" Emmet questioned.

She pursed her lips together and didn't turn to him, but

he saw the tears in her eyes. When her phone buzzed for the nineteenth time, she let out a strange cry and dug for it. She nearly chucked it into the water, when Emmet grabbed her wrist to stop her.

She shrieked and struck his chest. "Let me go!"

"Easy, Mara," he immediately dropped his hand from her wrist. "I'm not gonna hurt you."

Almost immediately, Mara's whole body shook and fell into him. Her scream was muffled by his shirt and she struck his chest, not hurting him. Shaking her head back and forth, she cried out and he felt the wet tears on his shirt. Hating it when women cried, Emmet wrapped his arms around her and held her close. No man should ever raise his hand to a woman, nor make her cry in fear. His jaw ticked as he gritted his teeth hard. If he knew who the bastard was, he would gather his brothers together, all of whom were raised the same way, and they would track him down. The man would wish he'd never met Mara when they were finished with him. His father always taught him how to treat a woman, with respect and love. Make her cry from joy not fear or pain, he would say. She should be cherished.

"I'm sorry," she said, her words interrupted by hiccups.

"It's all right," he answered. "I'm here. My sister-in-law went through something similar a year ago. But she is strong, just like you and she was able to get through it. Of course, she had me to help," he winked.

She laughed breathlessly. "You can't fight my battles for me, Emmet."

"No, but I can be here for you."

She gazed up into his eyes. He knew he should pull back, but when she licked her lips, he couldn't stop himself. Leaning down to capture her lips in a kiss, he waited to see if she would stop them. When she didn't, he closed his eyes, feeling just the briefest of touches when her phone buzzed three times in her hand making them both jump and breaking the spell between them.

What in the bloody hell am I doing? Emmet demanded. He pulled away so quickly, he worried she would fall. "I'm sorry, I shouldn't have done that. We should get back," Emmet said. *And quickly,* he thought.

"You're right, I'm sorry. I was feeling vulnerable and needed someone," Mara said putting her phone back in her handbag. "Thank you, Emmet, for not taking advantage."

"I would have, had your phone not dinged."

"I would have let you," she admitted. Heading to the driver's side of the car, she didn't look at him when she opened the door and got in.

Emmet sighed harshly, *not good,* he thought. The faster they got back to the dealer the better. He had to get Mara McGrath out of his head.

Benjamin watched from his car up the road as Mara and the redheaded giant got back into the cheap little red car. He nearly pulled out his gun from the glove compartment when he saw the man try to kiss her. She was his and no other man could ever have her. Ever since he saw her singing at that little pub in London, he knew he had to have her. When he got her the job, it was like he struck gold even if she didn't know his full involvement in her hiring. But after what she did to him, he looked forward to exacting his revenge.

Ducking down as they passed, he slowly pulled out and followed at a safe distance. Mara should never have crossed him, she didn't know who she was dealing with. She had it good. He always spoiled his women, gave them everything they wanted. He only asked for a little loyalty in return. *Loyalty...* he scoffed. She didn't know what it meant. He would be happy to make her feel the same desperation he felt. *Soon*, he thought. *Soon, it would be over.*

CHAPTER
THREE

Chloe found her way inside the office building. Recognizing Paddy from a long time ago, she called to him. He turned with a brilliant smile that faltered when he saw her.

"Chloe?" by the time he said her name, his smile had all but disappeared. "It's been a while."

"It has," she answered. "I didn't realize you worked here. I thought you were still at the Plaza."

"I am," he replied. "But it's the off season. Cutting hours."

"Oh, of course," she said. "You look good."

"Thanks," he replied tightly. "What can I do for you?"

"Is there a reason you are so abrupt with me?" she questioned. Sometimes she cursed pregnancy hormones, but not at that moment.

"What would you have me say?" he asked. "I saw what my friend went through when you married his best friend."

"What *he* went through?" she demanded. "You may want to reconsider your choice of words, Paddy O'Shea."

"I chose my words carefully."

"Then you are misinformed. I would be married to him right now if he hadn't ended it. So, I am unsure as to why you are treating me with such distain."

Paddy's brows furrowed for a moment but soon the cool mask of indifference settled on his features. "If you are looking for an apology, you won't receive one."

"I wasn't looking for either an apology nor condemnation, especially not from you Paddy," she said. "Now, I happen to be very tired and Emmet said there was a seat I could have to wait for them. If you can simply point me in the correct direction, I would be happy to get out of your hair."

"His office is right over there. I'm sure he wouldn't mind if you waited there."

"Thank you," she answered. "And for the record," she turned back to him. "Emmet cheated on me then broke up with me. Tom has always been there. I love him more than anything. I would appreciate it if you never said that to me again."

Paddy said nothing and she headed into Emmet's office. Tears threatened. She hated the ups and downs of her emotions. But Paddy used to be a complete gentleman. Rogue but gentleman, nonetheless. Shaking her head, it wasn't worth anymore time. She and Tom had been married for eleven years and she was happier than she ever dreamt. It wasn't worth the effort to correct Paddy's misconception, instead, she closed the door to Emmet's office and nearly gagged. His cologne hung heavy in the air and as much as she used to love it, now, with every other sense heightened, she needed some fresh air. Opening the door again, she breathed deeply, smiling when she caught herself thinking how Tom's cologne never smelled stale to her. Maybe she was over Emmet O'Quinn after all.

She looked over and saw water bottles on the side board beneath an expanse of cupboards. Grabbing a bottle, she jumped when something fell out of one of the doors overhead. Seeing it was something important with the return address of the DNA Diagnostic Center, she did not pry and opened the cupboard to put it back inside.

She froze when she saw an old photograph taped to the inside of the cupboard. Recognizing herself and Emmet both younger, standing at St. Stephen's Green smiling, a fond memory came over her, it was the day he proposed to her. Tom had taken the photo but as much as she tried to remember the details of that day, all she remembered was the day when Tom proposed to her. He was her future and Emmet, her past. But if the way he was looking at Mara was any indication, she may have to warn her sister about the effects he has on women and more importantly his player approach to everyone.

"Chloe," Emmet's voice caused her to jump. She turned and saw a questioning gaze reflected in his eyes. Realizing she was staring at the photograph taped inside the cupboard and still held the envelope in her hand, a flush of color rose to her cheeks.

"I'm so sorry," she muttered. "This fell out and it looked important, so I opened the door to put it back. I didn't mean to pry."

He nodded and his eyes turned down to the envelope in her hands. He swallowed unconsciously. Thanking her, he extended his hand to take the envelope from her. Shutting the cupboard door and heading to his wall safe, nothing gave his emotions away, but she knew him too well not to see the tension in his broad shoulders or the tilt of his head, signs he was apprehensive. Quickly putting the envelope away, he walked around to his side of the desk and Chloe turned to her sister, standing in the doorway. Mara's eyes were red, and Emmet had a clear mascara stain on his light blue oxford shirt as if he held her while she cried.

Knowing firsthand how Emmet's embrace could remove any demons around her, she gently touched her sister's arm. "Is everything okay?" Chloe asked her.

Mara nodded but said nothing. Her eyes gave it away. She had gotten another text. Keeping her sister's secret had been one of the hardest things when Tom had asked what was going on, but he understood the bond of blood and dropped it when she told him she was sworn to secrecy. Still, the texts were getting worse and Chloe worried it was only a matter of time before her sister's past caught up to them.

"So, Mara," Emmet said turning to them and bringing Chloe's focus back to the present. "Please sit. Do you like the car?" She nodded again and smiled slightly. "Then let's see if we can get it for you."

"Why the hell did you let her in my office?" Emmet demanded from Paddy after Mara left in her new car with Chloe following behind.

Paddy looked up, unfazed by his outburst. Luckily, everyone else that worked there had gone home for the day and it was just the two of them.

"Where else was I supposed to put her?" Paddy asked sarcastically.

"Keep her out here, put her in the waiting room but keep her the hell out of my office!"

"Afraid your little shrine was discovered?"

"You're an arse," Emmet replied.

"Of course I am," he sighed. "I'm the only one here you don't intimidate. And what is this about *you* breaking up with her?"

"Go to hell, Paddy," Emmet stalked out of the room and went outside. The fresh air stirred his bones and cleared his mind.

His initial thoughts ran to the envelope Chloe had found. Thank god she hadn't looked inside. No one could know what was in that envelope, yet. Hell, he didn't want to know.

Closing his eyes, he took another cleansing breath and pushed those thoughts aside. Turning to something far more complicated, Mara. Even though their meeting had been interesting to say the least, she had stirred something within him that lain dormant for over a year. She needed help and he wanted to be the one to support her. He wanted to know what happened to her. Before she left, he made sure to give her his card, stressing if she ever needed him, to give him a call. He would answer day or night. Her forced smile, then subtle side-glance to Chloe waiting a respectable distance, made him nod and take a step back. He would never want to pit sister against sister, but she needed to know he was there for her, as he would be for any woman in need. He may be known as a player but when it came to the safety of his ladies, he would drop everything to take care of them.

Checking his watch, he shrugged. *Close enough.* He had purchased his dealership from Old Larkin when he retired and added a maintenance garage, as the nearest one was in Bantry Bay. A couple years he had been in the red, but with good help and a good economy, he was turning profits left and right. So much so, he was going to need to hire another sales rep.

Heading back inside to tell Paddy to close up, he grabbed his coat and car keys. He needed a pint. Almost as if she knew, his phone rang *Born in the USA* as soon as he got into his car.

"Hiya beautiful, where have you been all my life?" He asked.

His sister-in-law Ness giggled on the other end. "Sorry, handsome, I'm taken," she replied.

"Pity," he lamented. Her laugh was music to him and lightened his mood tremendously. Over a year had passed since she had arrived on Ireland's Shore but the circumstances surrounding her time there under the Irish sky were well ingrained in his memory. Since then, she had married his youngest brother Sean and they were expecting their first child by the end of next month. "How you doing, *cailín*?" He knew she loved it when he called her *girl* in his native language.

"Oh, you know, just waiting for next month," she sighed.

"How is my nephew treating you?"

"He's been a bit active," she admitted. "But Sean has been marvelous. He's cleaning the house right now, making me put my feet up. I'm so glad we are having this little lad in the summer when Sean can be home with me."

"Good on him," Emmet smiled, grateful for the tenth time Sean had seen sense last year and married Ness instead of Trisha allowing him not only the happiness he so deserved, but the ability to keep his job at the county school, instead of moving to Dublin.

"But I wanted to call my *other* favorite Irishman and see how you were doing."

"I guess I can settle for second best," he chuckled.

"Second only to my husband and father of this little rascal. But I've put in some Shepherd's Pie, only to realize I made far too much for just the two of us. I thought you might want to come over," she offered.

"Oh aye, woman, you know the way to me heart."

"I try," she giggled again. "Have to keep my Irishmen happy."

"In more ways than one."

"Och, you rogue."

"I don't want to know why Sean always has a smile on his face every single time I see him. It's nasty," he teased.

She laughed even harder. "Stop! You're going to make me pee."

"More work for Sean," he replied.

"He loves me, but I don't think he'd be very happy cleaning up."

"Perhaps," he answered. "What time do you want me over?"

"When are you leaving work?"

"I'm actually in my car now."

"Oh, that's early."

"The day was strange."

"In a good way?"

"Ehm, no," he answered. "Which is why I could use a dose of my favorite girl."

"Well, it won't be done for another thirty minutes but that'll be enough time for you to get here and start a beer," she said.

"Sounds like the best night," he replied, starting his car. "I'll be there in fifteen."

www.ingramcontent.com/pod-product-compliance
Lightning Source LLC
Chambersburg PA
CBHW052009020726
47501CB00004B/1068